THE FORBIDDEN PORTAL

THE FORBIDDEN PORTAL

CHRONICLES OF THE UNWANTED PRINCESS™
BOOK TWO

J.L. HENDRICKS

MICHAEL ANDERLE

DISRUPTIVE IMAGINATION

THE FORBIDDEN PORTAL TEAM

Thanks to our Beta Readers:

Crystal Wren, Nicole Emens, Micky Cocker, Mary Morris, John Ashmore, Kelly O'Donnell, Larry Omans, Michael Baumann, Daniel Weigert, Rachel Beckman, Theresa Holmes, Jim Caplan

Thanks to our JIT Team:

Angel LaVey
Dave Hicks
Deb Mader
Debi Sateren
Diane L. Smith
Jackey Hankard-Brodie
Jeff Goode
Kathleen Fettig
Micky Cocker
Misty Roa
Paul Westman
Veronica Stephan-Miller

Editor
SkyHunter Editing Team

DEDICATIONS

Dedicated to all you dreamers out there.
Never stifle your imagination,
and never stop going after your dreams!

— J.L. Hendricks

To Family, Friends and
Those Who Love
To Read.
May We All Enjoy Grace
To Live The Life We Are
Called.

— Michael Anderle

CHAPTER ONE

M ia had heard about it so many times, but being there in person proved exhilarating. Even though the trip through the portal to the Vampire Academy was controlled, the glitz and glamor of the city even seeped into the basketball-like gym they were in now.

When she had first heard they would be attending a meet, Mia hadn't been interested. If an event didn't have something to do with martial arts or with practicing her newfound abilities and trying to harness them, she wasn't inclined to focus on it. But when her friends had mentioned they would be traveling through a portal to Las Vegas, Mia had changed her mind.

Before she'd made the trip through the portal, she'd been given precious little information about the nature of the meet. Now she sat with the Scooby Gang in the back row, near the top of the cavernous auditorium, looking down at the court in confusion. It appeared to be a regulation basketball court, but with gray mats surrounding the hoops and padding around each one.

"So, who are we rooting for?" she asked. She was peering down the row when it dawned on her that they all wore shirts bearing their school's logo, and Zander was waving a foam finger with it emblazoned on the side.

"That has to be a joke," Carson said, his voice a shocked monotone. "Tell me that was a joke."

Mia was quick to reply, "Of course, it was." She faced the court to hide her embarrassment. "I know it's our school, but I've never heard of this game before."

"You've never heard of slamball?" Vivi asked, her voice mocking.

"No. Sorry."

"It's all right. You're new," Luna said, interrupting before things became hairy. Vivi was a few seconds and another lilt in her voice away from Mia delivering a chop to her throat, and Luna must have noticed.

"Yeah. Let up, Vivi." Zander scooted a little closer to Mia. Now flanked on either side by him and Luna, she felt a little less alone, but still very much confused.

"So." Luna drew in a deep breath. "Slamball is kind of like an official fae sport, right? All of the different academies have a team, though unlike human slamball, which I think is a pretty under-the-radar sport to them anyway, this version allows for more...creative play."

"Yeah, for one, when we say full contact, we mean *full contact*," Carson piped up from the other side of the bench. His eyes, however, never left the empty court. Mia suspected he was going to explode from excitement the second their team took the field.

"Right," said Zander. "We are allowed to use some of our abilities while on the court. For instance, the vampires who are playing against us today, they are super-fast and super strong, and they will use that to their advantage. Also, some of them can fly a bit, or at least hover. See those gray things by the hoops on either side?"

Mia nodded. *Did he say fly?*

"Those are trampolines. The player with the ball can jump on one of those to try to dunk the ball or to get a better angle for a jump shot. They have to look out though," Zander said.

"Why?"

"Because of the full-contact," Luna said. "Slamball can be pretty brutal, and if you are mid-air, you don't have a whole lot of protection. Sailing through the air against a guy who can hover means he has the ability to wait on you and either steal the ball or just flatten you. And flattening people is encouraged."

"Even with students?" Mia asked.

Zander bobbed his head. "Perhaps even more with students," he said. "School pride is on the line. There are fouls you can get if you check someone in the back or something, but hitting them from the front or side—as long as it's not a kick or a punch or something—is fine. Each team has twelve people since it's an academic league, and they can substitute in or out at any time. Which is good since people get carted off hurt all the time."

"So, we are playing against vampires?" Mia asked. The rules of the game were interesting and all, but the idea that actual vampires were going to be on the court and that she was going to see them play a game was fascinating.

"Not the sparkly kind, sorry," Zander said, grinning. "These vampires are really meatheads who happen to be of the undead-drink-blood variety. Some of them are actually dhampirs, though."

"What's a dhampir?" Mia asked, feeling a bit like a four-year-old asking very basic questions in the back seat of a car like "Why is the sky blue?"

"Half-vampire," Luna said. "Sort of like us halflings. They aren't quite as gifted as the vampires when it comes to magical abilities, but they are still super strong and really fast. Plus, they don't fall for the traps like full vampires tend to. Vampires are really adept at wooing people, and at casting wicked spells and stuff that make people do their bidding. Dhampirs aren't subject to it, and many of them are resentful of vampires. Many of them will turn into a full vampire when they die as a human but otherwise live mostly ordinary lives. A number of dhampirs end up becoming vampire hunters, which is helpful for policing them since otherwise, vampires would just try to get away with anything and everything."

"Never trust a vampire," Zander said, lowering his voice. "I know that might seem a little bigoted of me, but seriously, those things are evil when they set their mind to it, and they do more often than not. Really powerful vampires can even woo dhampirs, and that makes them especially dangerous. Thankfully, you don't see those in any of the academies, and it takes so long to get that good you never see it in students. Even still, you want to keep an eye open around them. They have silver tongues and will do anything to get what they want whenever they want it."

So much information was coming at Mia that she sat in silence for a few minutes. It was the first month of her junior year, and her studies were already overwhelming. Being a part of the social life of a fae was exciting, but draining too. She didn't know what was expected of her in certain situations, and it all seemed so formal that she hadn't quite gotten the hang of it yet.

The hierarchies and social graces of the fae world were still so new that she hadn't learned much of any of them, and now vampire students were being thrown into the mix too. After a while, Zander stood to get something from the concession stand and asked if they wanted anything. After taking an enthusiastic and optimistic order from Carson, everyone else settled on a fountain drink.

"Need help carrying all that?" Mia asked.

"I would like that," he said, and his eyes met hers for a brief moment before they darted away.

Mia descended the long staircase to the main lobby floor and decided to ask a few more questions about the world she was now learning about. It was less embarrassing to choose one of them and limit Vivi's mocking, and Zander seemed to be an appealing prospect.

"So, there's *our* school and the Vampire Academy. What other schools compete in slamball?" she asked. They rounded a corner and headed down a hallway toward the outer rim of the building where she assumed the bathrooms and food would be.

"Well, our league is pretty small. There are eight teams, two from each of the four schools. Each team is supposed to be split evenly in terms of talent, but most of the time there ends up being an A team and a B team. Today's game is pretty important because it's our A team against the vampires' A team. They have gone undefeated so far this year, including beating our B team, and we only have one loss so far."

"Who did we lose to?" Mia asked as they turned the corner and found the line for concessions. The smell of hot dogs wafted up to her, and she became aware of the intensity of her hunger and of how long it had been since she had a hotdog at a game of any type. Today, she would rectify this obvious miscarriage of justice.

"The stinkin' shifters."

"Shifters?"

Zander nodded as he read the list above the window where uniformed kids around their age stood taking orders.

"Like werewolves?"

"Yes, and others. It's really hard to get a bead on one of them when they shift mid-match. Plus, they are ridiculously strong. One of our gunners broke his arm in a game against them last year, and he never played again."

"A gunner is a position on the team, right?" she asked.

"Yes," Zander said, turning his bright smile toward her. "See, you're getting it. The gunner is the main shot-taker. Sometimes you have two on the court at once if you really want to press, but most of the time, our team plays with one gunner and two stoppers, who do the defense work. He got absolutely creamed during the game last year, and it shattered some bones in his arm. Took him forever to be able to do simple spells again, and his parents forbade him from playing on the team again this year."

"That's awful," Mia said as they finally reached the window. By this point, her stomach was rumbling, and her desire for a hot dog had turned into a need for a much more elaborate meal. If she wasn't careful, her eyes would make decisions for her stomach that would rival Carson's long list. The girl at the window had disappeared into the kitchen area, which was populated by a group of large men, their skin covered in tattoos.

"So, there are the shifters," Zander continued. "And then us, the vampires and then the witches."

"Witches?"

"Yes, and they aren't normally that competitive, but they can play spoiler a lot. Last year their A team beat the shifters' A team in the last game of the year and gave us homefield advantage in the playoffs. We beat the pants off the shifters in that game, in no small part, I think because of the crowd. It was insane."

The girl at the counter reappeared, her expression weary, as though she would rather be anywhere else in the world. Zander gave her the orders, and Mia chimed in to add a hot dog, a soda, and, at last, a small curly-fry order to the mix.

"We only have one size," the girl at the counter said, her tone impatient. The line behind them seemed to have grown to epic proportions, and snap decisions were required.

"That's fine," Zander said. "I'll help you eat them."

"Order up," the girl said, and fries seemed to materialize above her shoulder as a hairy hand curved around her to sit them on the tray.

Another person came up with a caddy bearing four of their drinks and sat Mia's in front of her. She popped in a straw and carried all the drinks while Zander grabbed the tray as they moved away from the ordering window and went to pay.

As she tried to balance the drinks on the register area to reach into her pocket for her cash, Zander waved her off. "I got it, don't worry."

Mia blushed and grabbed the drinks again, almost spilling hers on her shirt. Which would have completed her embarrassment for the day and given Vivi all the ammunition she would need for a lifetime of torturous barbs.

"Do you play slamball?" Mia asked as they headed for the hallway that would lead them back to their seating area.

"I've thought about it," Zander said. "But frankly, we don't have time. I am far more focused on making our group the best it can be, and with us getting our fifth member late and you not really knowing anything about our world, it kind of puts everything else on the backburner."

"Oh," Mia said, keeping her eyes on the floor as they walked.

Zander must have realized what he had said because he stopped in the hallway. "Hey, that came out wrong. Look, it's not your fault you don't know anything yet, and it's not your fault I don't play slamball. Honestly, even if I had all the time in the world, I probably wouldn't anyway. I'm terrible at shooting baskets, and gunners are the leaders of the team. If I wasn't a gunner, I would be unhappy on the team, and if I *was* the gunner, everyone else would be unhappy, you know?"

Mia couldn't help but laugh a little. Zander grinned.

"Sorry, I didn't mean for it to sound like I blamed you. C'mon. Let's get this stuff up to our seats before the game starts. I think you're really going to like it once it gets going. It's super-fast-paced and a little chaotic, so not knowing what's going on is kind of the natural state of the audience sometimes. Are we good?" he asked.

Mia nodded, but she didn't look at him. She knew his apology was sincere and that he didn't want her to feel bad, but at the same time, she did worry about things like that. What if she was the reason the group hadn't advanced as far in their studies and practice as they should have?

What if *she* was the one holding them back? She wouldn't be able to shake that feeling until she caught up, and with so much to learn, it seemed impossible to get there.

All around them, music filled the air and, what sounded like air horns started blaring in every direction. The crowd erupted in cheers, and the lights dimmed, spotlights dancing all around the arena as Mia and Zander strode through the hall.

"Too late!" he said, a smile stretching across his face as he picked up the pace and began to half-jog to the entrance of the seating area. Mia took after him, doing everything in her power not to spill the drinks, taking extra care with Vivi's bright-red punch, which was sure to find Mia's white shirt if so much as a drop was spilled.

As they rounded the corner and stared up at the steps to find their seats, Mia sensed eyes turning in her direction. Some of the people in the stands who were cheering and smiling, met her gaze and their expressions faltered, their voices dropping. As she headed up the stairs behind Zander, she was all too aware that she was now the center of attention for many people. Very unwanted attention.

CHAPTER TWO

Mia sat in her spot between Zander and Luna and tried to focus on what was happening on the court. Music filled the stadium again as an announcer came over the speakers and introduced each member of the starting roster of the vampire team.

The vampires appeared impossibly frail, and Mia had to remind herself they possessed incredible strength regardless of their body type, and that their thin and lanky appearance was a way of luring people in. It was a glamour in a certain way, but more physical than a spell. As each member of the team made it to the sidelines, the tension on the visitor's side of the arena kept building.

When the music changed, and the school song played over the loudspeakers, the noise became deafening. The Scooby Gang surged to their feet, cheering for their classmates while their entire half of the arena joined them. Carson and Zander sang along at the tops of their voices, and Mia glanced at Luna, who was singing to herself and smiling.

Mia wanted to relax, and she allowed herself to enjoy the game, but every now and then, even while their team was entering the court, a student would look at her. Sometimes multiple faces turned, coupled with conspiratorial whispers and the occasional finger pointed in her direction.

Principal Elmhurst had tried to keep Mia and her powers a secret, which had turned out to be a miserable failure. As with any school where teenagers collected, gossip lurked in every corner of every hallway and at every lunch table. Word about Mia had spread through the academy, and now she was a secondary source of entertainment for many of the fae students at the game.

It angered her that everyone seemed to know her business, and now they were concentrating on finding ways to talk about her without making it obvious. She shifted on the bench, and Luna seemed to notice her discomfort. A quick scan of the crowd revealed a few heads turning, with some sniggering to be heard in the distance, even over the blaring speakers.

"Don't worry about them." Luna turned to Mia. "They're just jealous because you got into the coolest gang in the school."

Luna's smile was disarming, and despite herself, Mia relaxed. She didn't want to hide anymore. She didn't even want to strangle them. Well, not all of them. Maybe the original student who had spread information they shouldn't have, whoever was making sure everyone knew about Mia. She'd love to plant her fist through the face of that person and make sure the next time they went gossiping, they did it with broken teeth.

In reality, though, it could be anyone. Lots of people had been around the group and had seen her do things beyond her level of ability, both good and bad. If a teacher was spreading gossip, it would be snuffed out soon enough, and they might be fired for it.

If a student was responsible, then Principal Elmhurst had better hope she found them before Mia did. Expulsion would be a hell of a lot better than any number of the terrible things Mia could do to them without breaking so much as a sweat.

Below them, the game began and, despite the protective

screen between the crowd and the court, Mia was quick to learn it wasn't the only barrier. At one point, a fae gunner bounced up for a dunk and was hit by what appeared to be a lightning strike coming from a defender's fingers. A whistle blew the game to a halt, and the fae player landed halfway on the trampoline, his lower half bouncing up and curving over his torso before he hit the floor of the court hard.

"Oh, come on," Carson shouted at the court and surged to his feet, looking for all the world as though he was going to throw his chili-cheese fries at the referee. But he sat with a thud and stuffed a handful of fries into his mouth when the officials convened. Over the loudspeaker, the announcer informed the crowd of a penalty shot as the referees broke up, and the offending vampire earned a foul against him.

"How is that allowed?" Mia asked aghast. She would have assumed a lightning strike went a bit beyond a simple body check.

"Well, they aren't, technically," Zander said.

"It's a foul on the vampire defender," Luna piped up.

"He should be ejected," Carson snapped, the last word yelled at the court as he popped another fry in his mouth.

"Every player gets three personal fouls. It's kind of easy to get a foul called on you with the trampolines, but vampires don't worry about that as much because they can just float and don't need the bounce as much. They still technically have to bounce for a point to score, and they can't hover over them defensively, but they can control their ascent and descent much better," Luna said. "That vampire there just got themselves their first personal foul, but he probably thinks it was worth it. Lightning strikes like that are not expressly forbidden, you just catch a foul for it since it's considered part of their powers."

"It's like if one of us was able to do a force-push and knock one of them across the court, out of the way," Zander explained. "If the student is strong enough, they could pull it off and only get a penalty for it, but it's kind of a cheap way to play."

"I would think shooting someone with lightning is pretty cheap," Mia said.

"Extremely cheap. Low class," Carson muttered and sipped his drink. The straw gurgled as he reached the bottom, and he stared at the cup as if it had emptied itself by magic. "Great. What else can go wrong?"

On the court, the fae player was removed and replaced with a different one, who was allowed to take a penalty shot. As the referee blew the whistle, the fae raced for the first trampoline and bounced off, twirled to one side to avoid the outstretched arm of the defender, and dunked the ball hard. A roar rose from the crowd as the fae score went up by three, and their team tied with the vampires.

"Wait, what is there to stop fans from interfering with the game if vampires have the ability to shoot lighting?" Mia asked as the fae team took a time out.

"There's a protective shield around the court," Carson explained. "Really strong stuff. Keeps the magic in, and outside magic out. It also tempers spells, so witches can't just hex someone to death, and it allows the referees to police the game since they are granted extra power."

"Has anyone ever gotten hurt? I mean, worse than the guy who got hit by lightning?"

"Oh yeah," Zander said. "Especially in the professional leagues. People get knocked around a good bit, and the magic they use in the majors is less tempered by the judges since they are usually highly trained and exceptionally good athletes and spell casters. A couple of seasons ago, a witch was paralyzed when she got checked by a different witch due to a spell that was stronger than the poor witch expected it would be. It was big news. A bunch more regulations went into effect then, including in the Academic League. Hence the transparent plastic walls on the side to protect crowd members from errant blasts."

The more the rules were explained to her, the more Mia seemed to understand them, and she realized it was a mixture of hockey and traditional basketball. Maybe with a little bit of magic thrown in, but it gave it a pizzazz she was sure made it rather unique. The game picked up again, and the frenzied pace became dizzying. It was all Mia could do to keep up.

As the game neared the end of the first quarter, the score was tied, and the Fae Academy had held their own regardless of being down their best player. Despite her basic knowledge of how slamball worked and the pressure of the attention of people in the stands, Mia enjoyed the game and was becoming invested. She loved being part of something with her team. The quarter wore on, and she received fewer stares as students focused on the game. More unifying cheers rose, and she joined the crowd in trying to rally her team.

At one point, Carson cheered with such passion for a check by a fae player on the vampire who had shot the lightning earlier, his remaining fries had soared into the air and missed landing in Vivi's hair by an inch.

Mia was somewhat disappointed when the fries missed Vivi since it would have been a great way to even things out should Mia not make it through the night without a cola stain. Instead, Vivi shuffled away from Carson, moving so close to Zander that he shifted too, and his legs came into contact with Mia's.

As the quarter ended and a small break was called, Carson stood and left for the restrooms—he had finished off his soda so fast that he had ended up drinking half of Vivi's too. Vivi took the opportunity to go as well, leaving Mia with Zander and Luna.

"How do you like it so far?" Luna asked.

"It's really fun," Mia responded, her enthusiasm perhaps a bit more passionate than she had intended. "I really like it. It's like a few sports slapped together with that wizard game. What was that called? Quid-something."

Luna held up a hand, closed her eyes, and clutched the bridge of her nose with the thumb and forefinger of her free hand. "Stop. Stop right there. No."

"What?"

"I know exactly what you're going to say, and no, it is nothing like that. I mean, yes, the witches do whip out broomsticks occasionally, and there is a lot of throwing a ball through a hoop, but that's where the similarities end," Luna said.

"Well, there *is* a lot of magic involved," Zander said, but Luna shot him a glare, and he fell silent.

"Is it the movies you don't like?" Mia asked, unsure of Luna's reaction. "The books are really good if you didn't."

"No."

Zander laughed, and Mia turned to look at him. Luna was almost fuming, which was very unlike her, and Mia hoped she hadn't ticked off her new friend. She needed all the friends she could get in order to counteract Vivi and a school full of gossips.

"She hates that series. Don't let her get started on it," Zander said. "If you do, she'll talk your ear off about its 'simplistic and harmful representation of the magical community.' Right Luna?"

Luna didn't say anything, but her lips were pursed together in a tight line, and she turned to face the court. "Sorry, I was just notic—" Mia said.

"It's fine," Luna interrupted her. "It *is* kind of like that game. Just don't tell anyone I said that, okay?"

Mia broke into a large grin and nodded. "You got it."

Amiable conversation filled the time as the trio waited for Vivi and Carson. When they had returned, the whistle had blown to start the second quarter. Carson was carrying an entire drink caddy, and the expression on Vivi's face confirmed all four drinks were for him.

They stood so the pair could return to their places. Zander glanced at his friend and asked, "Staying hydrated, are we?"

"I don't want to have to get up again," Carson said. He fell silent, and the group focused on the game, their cheering wild and loud as the fae academy scored a point.

The game went back and forth, but the vampires always seemed to grab a lead and hold on to it, forcing the fae team to catch up. Every time the fae side gained a measure of momentum, a vampire player would body check one of the fae so hard they would need to be replaced for a short period.

Much like every game ever, the referees were the subject of the most criticism, at least on the visitors' side of the arena. There was a suspicion of bias toward the home team, that fouls weren't being called on vampires, not only not at the rate they deserved, but also not at the same rate they were called on fae.

It was enough that Mia sat there, elbows on her knees, and a few fingernails in her mouth as the final minutes of the game came closer to reality. The fae team was down by six points when a fae player managed to score a three-point shot before a fae defender stole the ball and made a two-point shot of his own. Before they knew it, they were down by a single point, and the vampire team took a time out with just over a minute to go.

"They're going to wind the clock down," Zander said through gritted teeth. "Man, we're going to lose."

Sure enough, when the whistle blew, the vampire team began to pass the ball back and forth, winding down precious seconds from the clock. It seemed like they would do it forever when a fae burst into the air, flying high off a bounce, and dive-bombed a gunner who was catching the pass. The ball shot loose, and a fae player grabbed it. He sped off for the hoop, bounced it high, and dunked it, tying the game.

"If we can hold them off, the game will go to overtime," Luna explained over the madness of the crowd's reaction.

The whistle blew as the vampire team received the ball,

sinking a two-point shot with ease, and they abandoned all hope. But, with a mere three seconds remaining on the clock, the fae team snatched the ball.

As the whistle blew, the fae guard tossed it to the gunner who took one step and jumped, and using his own side's trampoline to boost his height, he tossed the ball at the opposing hoop.

The ball appeared to soar through the air in slow motion and landed on the rim, circling it as the crowd held their breath. The ball hit the rim, and as it began to spin, the buzzer sounded, signaling time expired.

Mia rocked on her seat, her nails in her mouth as she chewed them and wished with her heart that the ball would fall in.

As though pushed from Mia's direction, the ball dove through the hoop, and the crowd went insane. Amidst the crazed cheers, the blaring music, and the announcer calling the game for the fae, Mia embraced Luna and turned to Zander.

The smile he beamed at her contained more than happiness. It held a question. Everyone seemed so sure that no magic could penetrate the court, and yet—

Mia smiled back at him as celebrations broke out in the auditorium.

CHAPTER THREE

Cinder felt like she was going to burst with excitement as she zoomed back to the academy ahead of the other students. Being a pixie had its advantages, and it allowed her a quick escape and fast travel through the portals on account of being so small she could not be seen.

A trained eye could spot a pixie, but Cinder made it more difficult by floating and swirling like a piece of dust unless she was in a hurry. Anything to blend in and make herself invisible so she could go where she wanted, whenever she wanted.

Not that her techniques worked all the time. Cinder's magic had a bad habit of backfiring and causing small fires. Enough of a reputation had built by now that whenever a fire broke out— even if in the kitchen and caused by the cooks—Cinder would be blamed. Which was so unfair. Though she couldn't deny that she *was* responsible, at most, half the time.

But today was special. Dan and Steve, the gargoyles of the Fae Academy with the odd names, had tasked her with a job of great importance. She was to follow the new student, Mia, into the portal and keep an eye on her while the halfling attended a game of slamball.

Considering that Cinder remained inside the academy most of the time, the prospect of heading to a different place and being around so many people had been exhilarating. She had accepted the job without hesitation and had zoomed her way through the portal as the last of the students had left for Las Vegas.

Now she headed back, excited, overstimulated, and bursting at the seams with pride at a job well done. Dan was her friend, much more so than Steve, and she was proud that he trusted her with an important mission, and prouder still that she had executed it so well.

With so much to tell him, she began to rehearse her report well before she made it through the portal. She had to keep track of all the information after all, so a little practice couldn't hurt.

As she entered the library, listening to the sounds of the first of the students making their way out of the portal and back home, she made a beeline for Dan, still talking herself through the practice run of her report. By the time she reached him, a minute or so earlier than she had expected, she was still babbling. The gargoyle cocked his eyebrow and waited for her to take a breath. It took a few moments.

"Cinder," he said, interrupting as she drew a deep, nervous breath in preparation. "Start from the beginning, little one."

"Oh." The pixie gave a tiny squeak.

Steve rolled his deep-set eyes. He had never trusted her, that much Cinder knew, but he also seemed to dislike anything he interpreted as silly, and Cinder was nothing if not a little silly.

"For the love of all that is fae, can you get her to calm down?" Steve snapped.

Cinder went still. She had been darting around and between the gargoyles, landing on their heads, and diving off, all while continuing to talk. "Fine," she said, grabbing the chain of a lamppost beside the library's entrance to hold herself still. "See? I can be still. I can stop."

"Good. That's wonderful, Cinder. Please tell us what you

found out," Dan said, his deep baritone voice bouncing off the columns of the library and against the entrance hall where the gargoyles stood, locked in place.

"Oh, Dan, it was so exciting! The fae team was getting beaten pretty badly by those dastardly vampires, and then one of them shot lightning." She inhaled while at the same time gasped to create an ear-piercing sound that made Steve roll his eyes again. 'There was a lot of back and forth and then, you'll never believe it, the game got all tied up! Then one of the vampires scored, and I was so sad, and I wanted so badly to punch his nose, but then a fae player threw the ball blindly in the air, and it went in! With no time left! It was incredible, and everyone cheered and there were people kissing each other, and I was so happy!"

She sighed and fell silent, having gotten the most pressing details of her mission out, and settled onto a nearby bench, her eyes twinkling lights in the dark.

"That's great, Cinder. However, we sent you there on a mission," Dan said.

"Oh! The halfling, Mia," she exclaimed. "Yes, yes, I watched her like a hawk," she said, placing her fists over her narrowed eyes, as though they were a pair of binoculars.

"And? We haven't got all day," said Steve.

"What else are we going to do?" Dan responded to him. "Play checkers? We're gargoyles, St—"

"Ooh, I didn't tell you about the snacks." Cinder interrupted them, overcome with the need to reveal more information. "They have the greatest-smelling food there and drinks so big I could fly down the straw and bathe in them if I wanted to. Not that I did. Or would. Never crossed my mind, actually. I am just saying I could if I wanted to. Which I don't."

"Cinder, plea—" Dan began to speak.

"Then there was all of that portal business. Do you know when you go through a portal, it takes a few moments to get your sense of balance back? I didn't know that. Not one of their portals anyway. I went through and,"—she made a sound with her lips similar to the noise a plastic container of food makes when the lid is popped off—"there I was, a floating pixie lost in the big cold world of Las Vegas, and I couldn't tell which way was north if I'd had a compass stuck up my—"

"Cinder! The girl!" Steve yelled, and Cinder stopped cold. Her face scrunched up, and she dropped her fists to her sides, her expression resembling either an angry baby or an evil flower.

Steve remained unaffected.

"The girl is fine," Cinder said, in a tone so dead, Steve had no doubt how much Cinder detested him at that moment.

"Fine" was a decent word for it too, she thought. Something kept her from describing Mia as "good" per se, but she couldn't put her finger on it. Since the moment she had first seen the girl, something had stuck out to Cinder and drawn her attention, even before the gargoyles had asked her to follow the halfling. There was something *elegant* about her.

Cinder couldn't quite work it out, but something about Mia spoke of royalty, and only one story had made sense. If the bloodline of Princess Violet was within Mia, it had to be diluted. By multiple generations, by the mixing with human blood, or a combination of the two, there was a distinct dilution in Mia, if it were true. In the two thousand years since Princess Violet had died, so much had changed that Cinder wondered if it was worth noting, or even possible. For now, she kept that secret to herself. No need to cause a ruckus, especially when that particular ruckus could get someone killed.

Even a pixie.

So she didn't mention it to Steve or Dan, or anyone else. Not yet, anyway.

Just before she began to recount the rest of the night's events, a student strode out of the library and turned toward the gargoyles. The boy laughed, his tone filled with derision as he walked up to Dan. "Hey, gargoyle, where would you find the definition for the word 'cretin'?"

Before Dan could dignify such a ridiculous question with a response, the boy smacked the side of the gargoyle and guffawed, which to Cinder sounded like the braying of a constipated goat.

"In a mirror!" the student answered his own question and fell into another fit of uncontrolled mocking laughter.

Rage built up within Cinder, and before she knew what she was doing, she was conjuring a spell in her mind. No one spoke to Dan like that, not in front of her. Not when she wasn't around to hear it either, for that matter. Dan looked out for her and had always been a friend, even when she was too difficult for others to handle. Plus, he had trusted her with a very important mission, one she hadn't finished telling him about yet.

The funny thing about Cinder and her spells was her reaction to them. While her spells were tame and more useful for mischief than any form of battle, she loved using them to wreak havoc on the lives of those who annoyed her. The downside to her powers was that it caused her to sneeze.

Her sneeze was the only way to discharge her magic and activate whatever spell she cast. She had to sneeze. It had infuriated her for a long time that such an involuntary action was the only thing separating her from her already-limited power, but she had grown accustomed to it.

The only problems she experienced these days were those unfortunate times when she was about to sneeze, and it wouldn't come. Which had caused several embarrassing near-spells. Conversely, her sudden sneezes had resulted in a few ill-fated, accidental spells. One of which Steve was still mad about. The academy staff had yet to remove all of the cake crumbs from his ears.

The sneeze was coming, and she knew it might be difficult to do what she wanted originally, so she changed plans. Things moved so fast in her mind that sometimes she didn't have time to settle on one thought before another came barging in, demanding to be heard.

The sneeze exploded from her nose with all the cannon-fire sound of a mouse's squeak, and the boy, who was now attempting to climb onto Dan's back, found himself hovering a few inches above the gargoyle.

"Hey, wait a minute. What's going on here?" he exclaimed, as he floated higher until he was suspended at least ten feet above the ground. His body began to turn in slow cartwheels, so his head was occasionally upside down and staring at Dan and Steve in horror and confusion. "You aren't supposed to use magic against us! I am a student!" he yelled, his face growing redder and more flustered as the blood rushed to his head. He resembled a horribly ugly balloon with its helium running dry, now spinning hopelessly to its final resting place on the ground. But Cinder wasn't moving him down anywhere close.

"It's not us," Dan growled at him. His voice was low and eternally repulsed, but Cinder knew the differences. This was as happy as his voice ever became. He was at least mildly amused.

"Serves you right, though," Steve chimed in.

"Let me down, you miserable relics! My father will hear about this, I swear," the boy screamed as he spun in slow-motion, his pudgy stomach now exposed as his shirt collected around his neck.

"I should hope so," Dan said, and the faintest noise that could be mistaken for a chuckle escaped him.

Cinder flew up to the boy, hovered behind him, and began to push him gently. Her pixie-dust was going to wear off soon, and when it did, she wanted him in a very specific place. A crowd of other students had filed into the hallway and were watching with interest as he floated farther and farther away, heading to a fountain long since filled with murky, filthy, moss-covered, water. It mostly existed to catch rainwater from the edge of the library roof, and now he was hovering over it.

With the slightest touch, Cinder pushed him once more as the dust ran out, and he dropped headlong into the disgusting water. Laughter erupted from the students watching the spectacle, and Cinder flew around Dan in excitement. The boy fumed as he crawled out of the fountain and ran off, embarrassed and angry.

"As you were saying…" Dan said, and Cinder giggled. "But this time, leave out the game."

"Right, so there was someone there that was worrying. Mia didn't seem to notice him at all, but he was certainly watching her. He tried to make it look like he wasn't, but as soon as I saw him, I knew he was up to no good. I followed him around, and I heard him say something to a vampire about enchanting students to keep an eye on the new halfling."

"Do you know who he was?" Dan asked.

"No, but he seemed pretty good at whatever it is he does. He ended up enchanting two of the students to keep an eye on her and report back to him."

"Who?" Steve asked, interested now.

It filled Cinder with immense pride that her spying skills had not only garnered so much information, but that Steve seemed impressed. "One of them was Marcus," she said and hesitated.

"And the other?" Dan asked.

She twisted the hem of her dress before answering. She hated this. "Hazel," she said at last. "I'm sure she has no idea she's doing something bad. She's such a nice girl, and I like her a lot."

Mirthless laughter rumbled from both Dan and Steve. Steve's was also derisive, and Cinder put her hands on her hips. To make matters worse, her nose started itching.

"How silly of you. You should know better, Cinder," Steve said, his tone mocking. "Half-humans are mostly worthless trash. They are mean, deceptive and rude, and giving them an ounce of your emotional attachment is unworthy of a pixie, or any other true fae. They are like those mean girl-people from that human film. Always looking for a way to hurt others."

"Now, you see here," Cinder said, waggling her finger at the pair. "First off, how do you know so much about human-world things when you never leave the Academy Library entrance? And second, I'd rather spend a day with a sweet half-human who has flaws, like Hazel, than an old, grumpy gargoyle like you, Steve."

"You're right," Dan said, sobering up. "Absolutely right. Humans and halflings can be much more than what we give them credit for. Specifically, this Mia. Cinder, I have another task for you."

"Another mission?" she said with an awed sigh. All her anger had disappeared, and she was vibrating with excitement.

"Yes. I want you to get close to Mia," Dan said. "Befriend her like you did Hazel. If things are going to go as I fear, she will need your help."

CHAPTER FOUR

"Okay, remember, try *not* to kill each other. Right, Mia?" Zander grinned at Mia. She returned the smile, and the group tightened up their circle.

They were practicing a simple spell to start, using their power to create a basic shield around them, a dome, impenetrable as long as they all focused. It was a rather easy spell, and something many of the students could do, albeit to varying degrees of strength or length of time. But Mia seemed to have trouble with it.

When it came to powers involving throwing, levitating, or growing things, she learned fast. They were all action-based, and one movement would feed into another. But her defensive skills remained far behind. It was as though she became bored and lost interest, or somehow the spell would become an active one, and things would get weird.

Like now.

As soon as the dome was above them, slowly fading inward, like a contact lens that appeared out of thin air, Mia's side began to discolor. No one noticed at first, until Carson glanced her way. He always kept an eye on Mia, watching for situations such as these. Zander gave her a lot of rope, enough to hang herself with, which would be fine if it weren't for the rest of them swinging by her side when she screwed up.

Carson waited only a moment until a yellow lightning bolt shot across her fifth of the shell. "Hey, Zander?" he said, almost beneath his breath.

Mia, whose eyes had been closed until then, opened one and looked around. The moment she saw the lightning, she squeezed them them shut.

"Yes, Carson?"

"Uh, I think Mia might be doing it again."

"Doing what, exactly, Carson?"

Zander's eyes were also shut, but not tightly. His lids were calm and relaxed, as was the rest of his body, and he exuded peace and confidence. This was a spell he could handle, and he firmly believed everyone else in his group could manage it, as long as he had enough faith in them.

Unfortunately, Carson was not so positive. "She's about to kill us all, for one," he said.

Zander's sigh was heavy. As he opened his eyes, Mia lost all control. Lightning shot up the side of her dome, zig-zagging in various patterns and ending up striking the ground over and over.

He watched the lightning and turned his attention to Mia. Her eyes were shut tight, and she seemed to be biting her tongue as she concentrated. The problem was when she tried to focus too hard, she made her powers—as chaotic as they were —stronger.

A bolt escaped the directional push she was sending them, shooting off the other side of the dome, and headed for the center. When the lightning reached the middle of the shield, it soared away, aiming at Vivi.

Zander cried out and ran to her, diving at her and pushing her out of the way at the last second. The bolt landed in the grass where she had been standing and destroyed it, lighting some of it on fire.

"Get off of me," yelled Vivi, who had fallen beyond the circle with Zander, into a wide puddle of mud.

Carson glared at her. "He just saved your lif—"

"And ruined my sweater! Get off," she yelled.

Zander stood, wiping mud off his own clothes and glanced at Mia, who was sitting on the ground, covering her eyes with her hands. He couldn't tell for sure, but she appeared to be crying.

"What was that, Mia?" he said, trying to control his anger and focus on how awful Mia must be feeling. Though, with as much as Vivi tortured her, perhaps she didn't feel quite that sorry.

"I don't know," Mia said, deep in her hands. Though her voice was muffled, her disappointment and despair were clear. He knelt close beside her and lowered his voice to a whisper so the others couldn't hear.

"Did you target Vivi on purpose?" he asked.

She lifted her face from her hands, and her makeup was streaked with tears. She looked deep into his eyes. He didn't need to hear her say it, but she was going to anyway. "No. I didn't."

Zander nodded and stood, turning to the group. "All right, so maybe I jinxed us before we started that time," he said. No one laughed at his joke. "How about we all just go on home and get some rest tonight and see each other for class tomorrow? Maybe some of us can cool off a bit."

His last comment was directed at Vivi, who was still fuming, though Luna had managed to get most of the mud off her clothes and from her hair. "If I see her again tonight, I am not responsible for what I do," Vivi said and stomped off.

By the time Mia had returned to the room, showered and dressed, Vivi was lying in her own bed, her sleeping mask emblazoned with "Princess" covering her eyes, and her headphones in. Luna appeared to be sound asleep, but Mia wouldn't get much rest that night. Not until the sun was almost over the horizon, and the new day was beginning.

It was mid-afternoon, and history class would be in full swing by now. Mia, who had overslept and was going to be ten minutes late for her first class of the day, was hurrying to the history room.

Vivi had hidden her alarm clock, and Luna had gone on her morning run before class, so it was by sheer luck that Mia had happened to wake up before the school day was over at all. She barreled into the class and glared at Vivi from across the room, but Vivi was beaming a megawatt smile at her.

"So nice of you to join us. Won't you please sit?" asked Professor Metabo.

Professor Metabo was a kindly old man, short and squat with tufts of white hair sticking out from random places on his head. He often tried to comb them into something resembling a normal haircut, but it was no use, and he was apparently far too prideful to shave it off.

His beard, on the other hand, appeared to be trying to compensate for the lack on top of his head. Long and yellowish-white, it was braided from his chest to his feet. The braid swept the floor between his legs enough that he often stepped on it. Mia took her normal seat beside Luna and opened her book, checking her friend's page and matching it.

"Now, who can tell me what the originals were for?" the professor said, pointing at a slide of a handful of artifacts on the screen above him. They looked like pottery from the ancient Egyptian era, and indeed one of them appeared to have a hiero-glyph carved along the bottom border. Vivi raised her hand high and had almost fallen out of her chair before the professor pointed at her.

"They were gifts from fae to humans to store magical power," she said with confidence before turning to glare at Mia again and flicking her hair.

Mia wondered if she could conjure those lightning bolts by herself right there and then.

"Yes, yes, exactly right," the professor said, interrupting Mia's train of thought. "The Egyptians were a fascinating people. They worshiped all kinds of things, and among them were fae. Yes, it's true. Many of the hieroglyphs have been misinterpreted to be about fictional gods created by fanatical priests, but in fact, many were fae creatures who, for their creativity and worship, gifted the Egyptians with power that would not be seen anywhere else on the planet."

"What kind of powers did the fae gift the Egyptians with?" Carson asked from the other side of the room.

Mia couldn't tell if he was genuinely interested or simply trying to get the professor to go off on a tangent as he often did, but either way, she was fascinated. It made so much sense. Of course, the Egyptians had received help from the fae, there was no other way to do anything they did.

"Well, I am glad you asked that, Carson. Very keen question. So, what we know is the ancient fae gifted the powers of glamouring, and we know what that is, don't we?"

The class, in a depressed monotone, muttered that they did. Professor Metabo seemed to take that as an affirmative, but apparently believed he should explain it just in case.

"Right, of course, glamouring is the act of changing a person's appearance, isn't it? That would be useful in battle, or espionage, or in the act of getting people to do your will based on one of their many gods, yes? They also used the power to create, and this is very important. The ancient Egyptians were capable of some very powerful magic of creation, thanks to the ancient fae. This included the ability to create monsters, which is where we have the basis for many stories of revenge of the Pharaohs.

Indeed, many of the pyramids themselves were cursed to contain some of these monsters to protect the dead housed inside.

"Speaking of the pyramids, do we know how they were built?" The professor smiled with glee as he awaited a response from anyone in the class.

Another general agreement was shared by the class, but this time it was more of a collective shrug. Most of the students paid very little attention in history class, and others were too sleepy from early classes and late lunches to care.

"The fae, of course!" Professor Metabo announced. "This is why no one has been able to recreate the ability to build a pyramid using tools available at the time. The fae helped them do so in exchange for the use of the pyramids. In ancient times, those pyramids would have stored raw magic, much the same way a nuclear plant stores energy. Both the humans and the fae would have benefited from this, and it truly altered the course of history for both."

Later, he assigned the class a reading portion, which Mia blew through in her voracious desire for knowledge of the fae world. She had long wondered how the early Egyptians could have created such wonders, and a secret pleasure of hers had been watching silly TV shows where they insisted aliens were the true masterminds. If only she could tell those people that the fae were responsible. Her mind reeled from all the stories she had believed she knew about human history and how many would have much simpler explanations if fae were involved.

Her mind wandered to other creatures she understood to be mythical. How many of them were real? The question gnawed at her until class ended, and she joined Carson, Luna, and Zander in the hallway. Vivi, thankfully, went in another direction, heading for the restroom, leaving Mia to join them without the temptation to rip someone's face off.

"Morning, sleepyhead," Zander teased.

"Vivi stole my alarm clock," she said, defending herself.

"We know," said Luna. "She told us right before class. I almost skipped it to come wake you up, but I really love all the history stuff."

"Me too!" Mia said, her response more enthusiastic than she had intended. "Especially since it's all new to me."

"Fae have been in secret contact with humans for a long time. It didn't end well for the ones who had open contact, like with the Egyptians. We will get to all that later in the course," Zander said, "But it isn't pretty."

"Can I ask you guys a question, but promise you won't make fun of me?"

"Yes," said both Zander and Luna.

"No," Carson said and chortled. "Kidding. Yes, go ahead."

"Werewolves."

They fell into silence as they walked, and Zander raised an eyebrow. "What about them?"

"Are they real?" Mia asked.

"Not anymore," Luna said.

"Get out," Mia said, elated to be learning this new information. "What do you mean, 'Not anymore?'"

"Well, wolf shifters are real," Carson said. He didn't mention it much to the group, but shifters were kind of his thing. He studied them intensively and enjoyed the lore in his spare time. "Werewolves, not so much. They were actually a problem at one time."

"Why?" Mia asked. Even Zander and Luna seemed interested. They may have known a version of the long story, but Carson was the expert.

Heat rose in his cheeks as he realized he was being put on the spot. "Well, you see, if a wolf shifter bites a human during a full moon, it creates a werewolf who is controlled by the chaos of the cycle of the moon. Which, of course, means the person has trouble figuring it out, and goes on rampages, and often ends up becoming a huge problem for everyone. So, it's been a law for a long time now that shifters cannot create werewolves."

"What happens if they do, though?" asked Mia, rapt with attention.

"There are hunters who have the job of finding and eliminating illegal fae and other creatures: Bounty hunters." Carson's eyes met Mia's, and the dawning realization clicked in her mind. "It happens every once in a while, that a shifter will turn someone into a werewolf, and it may take some time to find out. That's when someone gets called in to not only hunt down the werewolf and eliminate it but to do the detective work of finding out who turned them and eliminate them too."

"Eliminating them, meaning killing them?" Zander asked.

"Yeah. Kaput. Doneskis. Pushing up daisies. The thing is, werewolves are unpredictable and are stupidly strong. They aren't easy to hunt down since they look like a human most of the time, and when they are a wolf, they are so hard to catch and fight that it sometimes takes a team to get them." Carson scanned the group and spotted Vivi approaching.

"I had no idea," Mia said, her voice no more than a whisper.

"So? Practice later?" Carson said, changing the subject as Vivi reached the group.

"Yeah, I guess so, if everyone is rested and ready. How about you, Vivi?" said Zander.

"I'm fine as long as no one tries to murder me with lightning again," she said.

"I can't make any promises, other than next time, I might not miss," Mia retorted.

Vivi's jaw dropped while both Zander and Carson burst into laughter. Luna took Mia by the hand and led her away. Better to get to the next class than end on any other note than that one.

CHAPTER FIVE

"I think I'm just really tired," Mia said.

"Has that been your excuse the entire semester?" Vivi asked. "Because it seems to me this isn't a whole lot different than every other time we've tried to accomplish anything."

Mia shot her an angry glare, but it wasn't as if the dark-haired girl was inaccurate. They practiced constantly, shoving sessions in between regular classes and spending their evenings, and well into the night, trying to use their powers together.

But no matter how hard they tried or how often they practiced, they still hadn't accomplished their goal. Something always managed to go wrong, and more often than not, it linked right back to Mia.

Not that she didn't have the gifts of the other members of her group. In fact, they were learning this halfling's abilities were nothing short of astonishing, even beyond those of the four she worked with. But it wasn't the level of her abilities that mattered. The others possessed far more skill. They had trained and learned their entire lives, readying themselves for their education, and for using their magic as they grew older. She hadn't had that opportunity, and it was showing.

That night they stood on the soccer field behind the main academy building, trying again to combine their magic to create a stronger power. The Power of Five loomed over all of them, the potential of achieving something amazing, something no one would expect from young halflings. They all wanted it, but the flashes sparking from Mia's fingertips and the sudden gusts of wind that knocked them around didn't bode well.

"Just try again," Zander said. "It's not going to do any good standing around complaining. We need to keep trying."

"And you think *that's* going to do any good?" Vivi snapped.

Anger surged inside Mia. She was furious at Vivi for the way she constantly ground into her, occasionally giving her only enough of a break to make her think their relationship might start smoothing out, only to snap back. Mia was always left a little off balance and unsure of herself.

She was angry at the forces keeping her from knowing who she truly was, that were putting her through the struggles she was facing now. And she was angry at herself for being unable to catch on the way she wanted to.

She had never struggled this much before. She had always been good at what she did, building skills and mastering abilities with ease. It was exactly that way with her Wushu training. She had excelled almost from the first moment she had begun her training. She was accustomed to being the best.

And then she had come to the academy.

Her anger grew stronger, and the sky went dark. Heavy clouds rolled in from all directions until they covered the moon and stars. All light disappeared. A deafening crash of thunder split the air, accompanied by impossibly bright lightning. It looked like the entire world had caught fire in a second.

When her eyes recovered from the flash, she saw that the whole world hadn't caught fire. Unfortunately, several trees surrounding the soccer field were burning. Lit by the lightning, the trees blazed, flames jumping onto other branches, the fire spreading around the edge of the field.

In the next instant, the clouds broke open, and torrential rain fell on the soccer field. Mia checked the academy building—maybe it was contained, like in the dome in the field at the edge of town. But the rain was also pouring down on the building.

Perfect. This time, she had managed to create a catastrophe that affected not only their practice field but the entire school as well. The Scooby Gang shouted and ran around, flailing as they screamed at Mia to stop the rain which was coming so fast the ground couldn't absorb it.

Puddles had already formed, and the water became deeper with every passing second. Mia tried to stop it, but her efforts only made the rain come down harder.

The others ducked their heads, trying to find a spot away from the deluge so they could breathe. Mia heard them sputtering and gasping. She concentrated as hard as she could, and the rain stopped.

Zander stared at her, his hair hanging in his face, water dripping from his nose and ears. "Well." He gestured toward the edge of the field. "Here's a silver lining. At least the rain was hard enough to stop the fire on the trees from spreading out to the rest of the grounds and to the building."

Mia smiled, but Vivi quickly wiped it away. "Silver lining? You see that as a silver lining? Oh, fantastic, the useless one almost drowned us all, but she didn't actually burn the entire place down, so yay!"

Mia turned to say something to Vivi but fell silent. Professor Elmhurst was hurrying across the field toward them. Mia straightened her spine and tightened her shoulders. She hadn't been aware that the headmistress would be watching their disastrous practice session.

Not that it should have come as any surprise. The principal had become increasingly invested in the team's progress. It was like the harder a time Mia had, the more Elmhurst focused on pushing them to the next level.

"Well, that was quite the display."

This was perfect. Not only did Vivi have to endure the frustration of being a part of these disasters, but now she faced the humiliation of knowing Elmhurst had been watching. The headmistress studied each student, taking in their sopping clothes and the hair stuck to their heads.

"I need to have a talk with you," Elmhurst said. "I've been watching your practices, and I can see that Mia's skills are out of control. You have the ability, Mia. You just aren't focusing enough to make it happen. You haven't gotten control of those abilities. You haven't put them at your own disposal. But I'm telling you, it doesn't have to be that way. You can do anything you put your mind to."

Vivi scoffed and rolled her eyes before she could hold back the reaction out of respect for Elmhurst. But Vivi hated these special after-school pep-talks. More than that, she hated being unable to escape them, or the halfling they were directed toward.

Mia was an absolute pain, but unfortunately, she was also the only chance they had of attaining the Power of Five. Without Mia, they were going nowhere. At least, nowhere big. Nowhere that mattered.

Which wasn't good enough for Vivi. She wanted to be recognized as the very best fae of either Court. It didn't interest her to only be the best Unseelie halfling. She wanted to be known as the best halfling ever born, maybe even on par with mature fae in power and skill.

It had been a dream, something Vivi had always thought about but hadn't believed could ever happen. Not until Mia came around. Now that Vivi had seen some of what the halfling could do, she believed she was witnessing the possibility unfolding in front of her.

This halfling had the chance, too. But that only made Vivi

more driven and confident. Mia couldn't be the only halfling to possess so much power. It didn't make any sense. Vivi had to have more abilities and skill than Mia did. The other girl hadn't even grown up with training, so she couldn't possibly be better than Vivi.

"Maybe she'll never be able to control it," Vivi said.

Elmhurst shook her head. "No. That's not the case. She has to keep working on it. Remember, she hasn't been to school among fae since she was little the way the four of you have. Young fae learn their control the same way people learn language. They're exposed to it, and it just becomes a part of them naturally. Mia didn't have that chance, so now she has to work to gain, and maintain, that control. That's why you're going to work on it with her."

"Us?" Vivi asked incredulously.

"What do you mean?" Luna asked. "How can we help Mia learn to control her abilities?"

Elmhurst turned to Mia again. "I want you to concentrate on something small. Just a small enchantment, something you feel comfortable doing. Now, the rest of you will help her learn how to focus. That's the problem. Not that you don't have the abilities or even that you don't have the control. You simply haven't learned to master it yet. I believe you lack focus, and that's why your powers keep going haywire like they do. I've watched many of your practices, and it always seems to go the same way. You seem to have it and are doing well, then everything just—"

"Goes funky?" Mia asked.

Elmhurst laughed. "That's one way to put it. But you can get it. You can learn to find that focus and maintain it so you can sustain the power. It may not be easy. But you can do it."

Mia nodded. Vivi rolled her eyes again when the other halfling girl drew a deep breath as though preparing herself for the challenge ahead.

"She's not asking you to use your mind to pick up the building and turn it around," Vivi pointed out. "Just something easy."

"How about wind?" Carson asked. "You really seemed to get that the last time we worked with it. At least, for a while."

"Perfect," the headmistress said. "Nothing extreme. Just pick up a nice wind and keep it going. The rest of you distract her."

Mia faced the field and closed her eyes. Vivi shouted her name, and Mia whipped around to glare at her through narrowed eyes.

"What?" Vivi asked. "We *are* supposed to distract you, aren't we?"

"Vivi's right," Professor Elmhurst said. "She's not going to learn to focus if she doesn't have to fight distractions. Everybody, try to break her concentration. Mia, you have to try to block it out. Fight the frustration. Don't let it get to you or stop you from doing what you need to do."

Vivi couldn't help but smile. This was fantastic. Usually, she was hassled for doing anything that might distract the others or keep them from being able to use their abilities. Now, Professor Elmhurst was telling her to do exactly that. She could heckle and aggravate Mia, and no one could say anything to her.

It took some time, but finally, Mia began to get the hang of things. Even as Vivi and the group were doing their best to distract her and break her focus, she managed to take hold of her abilities and keep them under her command.

She created a light wind and kept it flowing over the practice field for five minutes, before discharging it smoothly. Nothing bad happened. No rain burst from the sky, and none of the trees flared up, either.

Satisfied at the progress, the headmistress strode away. Mia turned to the group with a triumphant smile, and Luna grinned at her. Zander offered his congratulations, and Carson also appeared somewhat impressed. Vivi wanted no part in the little congratulatory party, but the others wouldn't allow her to go inside.

Now that Mia had more concentration and focus, they wanted to try again. For the next three hours, they attempted all of the spells they had done before. Faerie circles burst from the grass, they played with wind, and she was able to create a small, concentrated storm which she could pass from person to person without risk of drowning.

Finally, the group was tired and ready to call it a night. Mia was gaining control, and they were excited to keep pushing and discover what she could accomplish.

"Why don't we meet up early tomorrow?" Mia asked. "Right after classes."

"Sounds good," Luna replied. "Let's meet up outside the library."

Since two of their group had the last class of their day at the library, it was the most central location to meet. All five agreed and returned to the academy building to get something to eat and get some rest.

CHAPTER SIX

"I don't know. Do you really think that has anything to do with it?" Mia asked, leaning against the wall.

"Absolutely. She has a major complex about being in the Unseelie Court. Having a half-brother in the Seelie Court just drives her crazy," Luna said.

"But he's only a baby. How could she be that offended by a baby?"

"He's a baby now, which means he's super adorable and everybody is falling all over themselves for him. But he's going to get older, and when he does, being in the Seelie Court will become a thing for him. It's already embarrassing enough for her to be a halfling. But to be a halfling with a human father who now has children with two different fae women, one Seelie and one Unseelie, just feels like a complete scandal to her."

"Is it a scandal?" Mia asked.

Luna laughed and shook her head. "Not really. There are a few people here at the academy with half-siblings or step-siblings. Some even have half-siblings who are full human, and some have half-siblings who are full fae. There are some people who have terribly strict rules about the Courts and what is and isn't okay, but there are a lot more halfling families like that than there are regular mother, father, half-kids."

Mia shuddered. "I know what you meant, but 'half-kids' is not a visual I needed."

Luna chuckled. The two halfling fae girls were standing outside the library waiting for the group. They had finished class a few minutes early and had been standing there for a while.

Their conversation had led to a girl in one of their classes, a particularly strange halfling called Sage. She wasn't strange like Vivi, but more a theatrical, melodramatic type of strange. That day she had disrupted class with a long-winded, repetitive speech about oppression that left everyone in the class wondering who exactly she believed was being oppressed. Her words turned back on themselves so many times she had ended up contradicting herself in at least three ways.

Above the two girls, Dan and Steve were listening to their chat. They had been eavesdropping since the pair had arrived, but hadn't said anything. The two gargoyles were doing their best to keep their distance from Mia.

Since their conversation with Cassia, they hadn't spoken much to Mia but had done their best to keep an eye on her as promised. They preferred to watch over her and ensure she was doing fine, but without making it obvious to her, or to anyone else. The gargoyles didn't want any of the students or the faculty to suspect that they liked Mia. They didn't want anyone to think they had any interest in her. That would accomplish nothing but put a big target on her back.

Everyone would wonder why the two curmudgeonly gargoyles were fond of the new halfling. Which might make them look closer at Mia and try to figure her out. Steve and Dan definitely didn't want that. It would put Mia at risk and upset Cassia.

Besides, it would hurt the gargoyles' rep if anyone at the academy discovered they might possibly be nice, or that they actually liked anyone. That would ruin how people saw them. All the students believed the gargoyles were mean spies for the faculty, which was how Dan and Steve preferred it.

Vivi was in a particularly good mood as she approached the library a few minutes later. At least, Vivi's version of a good mood. The practicing in the soccer field the night before and Mia's disaster had inspired a new prank, and Vivi had spent all day mastering it.

Although the near-drowning in Mia's massive storm had made Vivi miserable and ticked off, tossing the smaller storms around later had been more amusing. Which had given her the idea to drop a storm cloud over the heads of the two nasty-spirited gargoyles perched outside the library. But she wasn't simply going to stop at that. As soon as the rain started, she was going to create a bubble around each of them so it would fill with water and drown them.

Her plan sounded far more dastardly than it really was. They weren't going to drown. A little water wasn't going to kill them. It couldn't. Steve and Dan weren't really alive. They were merely animated statues. Since they didn't breathe, they could remain underwater for as long as she wanted, and it wouldn't be a problem. At least, it wouldn't be a problem for them *physically*. But it would certainly aggravate them.

One thing Vivi had learned about the gargoyles early on in her time at the academy was that Dan and Steve hated water. Being permanently attached to their posts outside the library meant constant exposure to the elements. No matter what was going on with the weather, they were out there in it.

They were rained and snowed on throughout the year, and they could do nothing about it, not even shake to get the droplets or snowflakes off. After countless years spent on campus, the two hated anything other than sunshine.

Vivi positioned herself at the perfect spot so she could watch without anyone, particularly Mia and Luna, seeing her. She conjured the storm cloud and positioned it right above the gargoyles. The dark cloud grumbled and broke open, sending a deluge of water down on the statues and the surrounding area of the building.

On the other side of the statues, Luna and Mia glanced up at the sudden rumble of the storm and ran inside to get out of the cold rain.

"Where did that come from?" Mia brushed away the water still clinging to her clothes. "It was sunny just a minute ago."

"I have no idea," Luna replied. "That came out of nowhere."

Out of the corner of her eye, something caught Mia's attention. She glanced out the windows across the library and waved at Luna to get her attention. "Look at that," she said.

They went to the window and peered outside. There was no sign of the rain. Beyond the glass, the day was bright and sunny.

"What's going on?" Luna asked.

"I don't know." Mia shook her head. "Let's go find out."

They hurried to the other door of the library and ran out around the corner of the building to where it was still sunny. A distinct line marked the sky where the clear weather ended, and the storm began. And Vivi was standing behind a column and laughing gleefully.

Mia turned her attention to Dan and Steve. Water was collecting around them in a bubble. The gargoyles were gurgling and shouting, struggling as much as they could without being able to move. They were drowning, and a surge of fear tightened Mia's chest. Terrified for their safety, she ran across the yard toward the rain. She didn't have time to think about anything. Without considering what she was doing, she waved her hand at the gargoyles.

With a loud popping sound, the invisible bubble surrounding the gargoyles burst, and all the water gushed down. Vivi was perfectly positioned for the entire wave to splash onto her. Her scream was high-pitched, and she raised her arms, but she wasn't fast enough to stop herself from being soaked from head to toe.

Carson and Zander approached Mia with Luna in tow, just as the water fell onto Vivi. Mia was still shaking with worry and wrapped up in her effort to save the gargoyles, but the boys instantly burst into laughter. The amusement helped break Mia from her thoughts, and she saw how hilarious Vivi looked, standing there sagging and dripping like a drowned rat.

Vivi released an angry, exasperated sound, somewhere between a growl and roar, stomped her foot, and whipped around to march off to the dorms.

"You better run," Dan shouted after her.

"Watch your back, Vivi. We're going to get even!" Steve added.

They were spitting mad, but at least they were safe. Mia rushed to the pair and stared up at them. "Are you all right?" she asked. "Dan? Steve? Are you okay?"

"We're fine," Dan said flatly, his gaze following Vivi until she disappeared from view.

"I'm so glad," Mia said. "I was so worried you were going to drown."

The gargoyles looked down at her for a few seconds, staring as though they believed she was going to say something else.

"Oh. You really did?" Steve's eyes were wide, apparently surprised by the sentiment.

"Of course. You were completely underwater," she said.

"That's really nice. But we can't actually drown. We can't die. Vivi might be many different kinds of horrible, but she hasn't been murderous...yet. She just wanted to torment us," Dan said.

"Oh, well...I guess you didn't need to be rescued, then." Mia was embarrassed by her frantic reaction, trying to save the lives of beings who weren't actually alive to begin with. But the gargoyles' expressions were almost tender.

"No. Thank you," Steve said. "However, we can't stand water, and Vivi knows that, which is why she did it. She wanted to watch us be miserable. Who knows how long she would have kept it going if you weren't there to stop her? We're very grateful. And we absolutely owe you a favor."

Luna, Zander, and Carson gasped and exchanged amazed glances. They rushed toward the gargoyles, eyes wide.

"I have never heard of the gargoyles granting favors," Luna said to Mia.

Carson went right up to the statues. "Hey, if I knew you were going to be giving out favors, I would have stopped everyone from playing pranks on the two of you guys a long time ago."

The gargoyles promptly spat water at him. Mia joined in as everyone burst out laughing. Carson wiped the water from his eyes, and they walked around to the back of the library on their way to the practice field.

Mia stopped halfway there. "Wait. If the gargoyles aren't alive, and can't move, how is it they can talk and spit water?"

Luna shrugged and looked at the group. No one was offering up an explanation, so she did. "It's magic. Who knows how they do what they do, they just do it."

Mia's brows furrowed in confusion. "I don't know if I'll ever get used to this new life."

The gang laughed with her, and they continued their trek to the practice field, short one member.

"Do you guys actually think Vivi is going to show for practice?" Luna asked.

"I doubt it," Mia replied. "She's bitter enough about having to practice with me in the first place. She's not going to do it after being humiliated like that."

"But there's no point in us going out to the field and practicing without her. You can't exactly accomplish the Power of Five with only four people," Carson said.

"That didn't stop Professor Elmhurst from trying to get the four of us to do it," Zander pointed out.

"True. But that's not the point now. We're supposed to be

combining with Mia. We need Vivi if we're going to practice," Luna said.

"Just give her some time to cool off. She'll get over it. Why don't we all take the afternoon to catch up on some schoolwork, then we'll have dinner and see how she is after that," Mia suggested.

"Sounds good," Carson said. "I'll bring her down to the practice field after dinner. I'll be more convincing than the three of you."

CHAPTER SEVEN

"This is ridiculous, you know?" Vivi asked as she and Carson walked from the main academy building toward the practice field. "I don't need you to be my babysitter."

"I'm not your babysitter," Carson said. "I'm your escort."

She laughed mirthlessly and rolled her eyes. "Because that is just so much better. I also don't need you as my escort. I'm a big girl. I can get to practice on my own."

"Oh, really? So, if I hadn't come up to your dorm room and found you sitting on your bed pouting in your sweatpants, you still would have come?" he asked.

"I was not pouting. I was studying."

"Right. Whatever you were doing, if I hadn't shown up, you're telling me you would have willingly, and under your own volition, taken off those sweatpants, put regular clothes back on, and come down to the practice field to meet up with the rest of us?"

Vivi flashed him a glare. "Shut up."

The pair turned to go past the library, taking the fastest route down to the practice field, and they figured the other three were probably already there waiting for them. As they approached the library, a chorus of angry words was hurled her away. The gargoyles were shouting at her, yelling, and spouting what she could only assume they believed to be insulting curses.

The years they had spent stuck in one place had taken some of the modern edge from their insults.

"You dastardly buffoon!"

"You blunderbuss!"

"Cow-handed cabbage head!"

"Fop-doodle!"

"Fribble!"

"Ginger-snap!"

"Rattlecap!"

Vivi stalked toward them, glaring up at the statues. "You're slipping into rhyme, you idiots," she snapped.

Dan squirted water at her, and when she cried out and jumped away, Steve followed suit. They both followed up with a bigger squirt, soaking her shirt and the front of her skirt.

She growled angrily at them. "I can't believe you did that! I already had to change my uniform once today, thanks to the two of you!" she snarled.

"Thanks to the two of us?" Dan asked incredulously.

"You're going to blame *us* for that?" Steve asked.

"I ended up soaked," Vivi shouted.

"Because you thought it would be funny to put a bubble around us and have a storm fill it up."

"You can't even take a joke. That's why no one around here likes you. You are nothing but miserable chunks of worthless stone."

"At least we have being stone as an excuse," Dan shot back.

Letting out another angry, exasperated cry, Vivi lashed out at them, freezing them into place with a blast of magic. Instantly, they couldn't move what little bit they could or talk. The two gargoyles had been able to move their heads around before, but now they were totally stuck. And bits of ice hung from their stone bodies. Steve had a three-inch icicle suspended from his nose. While tiny, razor-sharp icicles dangled from Dan's eyebrows.

The only thing they could do was move their eyes around in their frozen faces. A furious shout from behind Vivi made her whip around. Mia was running toward her, with Luna and Zander close behind. Apparently, they hadn't had as much of a head start down to the practice field as she expected.

Mia couldn't believe what she was seeing. Actually, she could, and that just made it worse. Vivi had been tormenting the gargoyles again, and she had *frozen* them. Ticked off that the bitter Unseelie was hurting them again, Mia stormed up to Vivi and confronted her. "What is wrong with you?" she demanded.

"Excuse me?" Vivi narrowed her eyes.

"Don't try that. Don't act like you don't know exactly what I'm talking about. What amuses you so much about tormenting Dan and Steve? Is it just because they're easy targets? They can't defend themselves, so you bully them because it's fun? Or is it because they can't really do anything back to you, which is the only reason you would be brave enough to be as nasty to them as you are?"

"Watch your mouth," Vivi said through gritted teeth.

"Or what? What are you going to do to me?" Mia stabbed a finger at the gargoyles. "Look what you did to them. What is it, Vivi? They were so much of a threat to you because they could move their heads and speak? That's all they had, and you took it from them just out of spite. How could you do something like that? You've always been mean, but how could you do something so horrible to creatures who have literally never done anything to you?"

Vivi shook her head, and Mia was surprised at the shame flashing across her eyes. Vivi stared up at the statues before turning to Mia. "I didn't mean to. Really. I know you don't believe me, but I didn't mean to freeze them. I was angry, and it just happened."

"Have you ever done something like this before?" Zander asked. "How long is it going to take to wear off?"

Vivi shrugged, her expression growing more helpless. "I don't know. I wouldn't even know how long it would take for a spell to wear off when used against a gargoyle. It might not last as long as it would for a living being. It might last longer. I don't know."

In the next instant, the librarian rushed from the building and stalked toward them.

"What is going on out here?" she asked.

"It's me," Vivi said. "I got angry at the gargoyles and froze them."

The librarian's mouth fell open, and she glared at Vivi for a few seconds before she was able to bring herself to speak. "Fix it. Fix it right now. Reverse the spell," she demanded.

Vivi turned to the gargoyles and focused on them. She muttered a few words and shot her hand toward them, but nothing happened. "I can't."

"What do you mean you can't? You did it, now reverse it," the librarian said.

"I know I did it, but I can't reverse it. I tried. For some strange reason, I can't make it reverse."

"You need to figure something out."

Vivi shifted uncomfortably, looking between the ground and the statues. The energy around the group was anxious and on edge, all waiting for something to happen.

"I don't know what to do," Vivi said, sounding worried. "I didn't mean for this to happen. Really, I didn't. I'm sorry. If I knew what to do to fix it, I would. Honestly. I just don't know what to do."

It was the first time Mia had seen the girl feel bad about anything. Her head hung, and she appeared to be truly remorseful. But Mia couldn't bring herself to care how the other fae girl was feeling. All she could think about was the gargoyles. Her heart was breaking. She knew how much they were suffering and how horrible this would be for them.

Her eyes slid up and down Dan's face, and she wished he would be free of Vivi's spell and able to move off the pedestal he had been standing on for so long. No sooner had the thought flitted through her mind, than the air snapped loudly and the gargoyle fell forward off his pedestal and onto the ground.

The earth shook at the impact, and Dan blinked. A second later, he began to move. It wasn't smooth, controlled movements like a human, but Dan wasn't a human. He was a statue. And now, though, he was a statue who could move and talk.

The librarian and the Scooby Gang slid their eyes over to Mia, before shifting their attention to Steve. The group dissolved into questions and chattering.

"Aren't you going to move, Steve?" Luna's voice rose over the rest of the noise. "Come on. Just like he did. Just get down."

"Can't you do it?" Vivi asked, actually sounding hopeful. "Dan did. Try it. Maybe you can, too."

Professor Elmhurst looked around. A large crowd of students fanned out, gathering in the library yard. They all stared in shock and surprise at Dan lying on the ground and were all talking over each other.

There were so many voices and words that Mia couldn't pick any out specifically. It was beginning to overwhelm her, and she couldn't imagine what it would be like for the gargoyles. Steve hadn't responded to their questions, or to his companion who had toppled from the pedestal. He wasn't speaking or moving, which meant he was still frozen. If he wasn't, he would have at least said something.

Dan pleaded with her. "Please, Mia. Help him. Do whatever you did for me. Help Steve get down too."

"Mia, what happened here?" Elmhurst asked.

"I don't know." Mia shook her head. "I was worried about them, and the next second, Dan was off his pedestal."

"Do it again," Dan said. "Whatever it is you did when you were worried about me, do it again."

"I can't. I don't know what I did. I don't know how I did it."

"Please," Dan said again.

Mia looked at Elmhurst desperately, and the headmistress gave a weary sigh. "I don't know if this is a good idea. The gargoyles have been at their post since the very beginning of the academy. This is where they belong. But I'll help you."

Mia heaved a sigh of relief. "Thank you."

Elmhurst gave her a few instructions, helping her to refocus on the magic within her and turn it onto the remaining frozen statue. But nothing was happening. She repeated the process several times, but Steve stayed firmly in place.

A few failed attempts later, Steve had turned cotton-candy pink. He still couldn't move or speak, but he looked lovely. The next attempt removed the coloration from him, but still did nothing to get him off his pedestal. The next covered him with a variety of brightly colored feathers. The poor gargoyle seemed better off before she had started messing with him. Finally, she made one more attempt. A slight cracking sound preceded the gargoyle loosening from his place, turning sharply, and falling backward.

The crowd around her gasped, and a few students grabbed her shoulders to shake her. She was sure it was meant as an encouragement, but it was merely another layer of being overwhelmed.

"That's amazing!" someone exclaimed behind her.

"Did you see that?"

"Could they always do that?"

"How did she do that?"

"What does this mean?" Zander asked.

"Dan, Steve," Elmhurst said, pointing at each of the gargoyles to make sure they were paying attention to her. "No matter what just happened, you are to remember that you are still gargoyles. You have a duty."

"Are we?" Dan asked. He shifted, and the movement made him rise up off the ground a few inches. He gasped and glanced at Steve.

The other statue performed the same movement and rose up, too. "We can fly." Steve gasped.

Dan hit the ground and bounced up. Steve followed close behind him. A second later, the stone on their backs made a cracking sound, and their large wings opened, spreading out to the sides so they could fly higher. They made gleeful sounds and soared up higher into the air, swooping and flying in circles.

Mia couldn't imagine what it was like for them. For their entire existence, they had been stuck in place, standing on the same pedestals. They could move their heads and speak, but never anything else. Now they could not only move, but they could also fly.

She watched them happily, thrilled at the sight of them trying different formations and playing with each other in midair.

"Everyone. It's getting late. Everyone back to your dorms," the headmistress announced loudly. The crowd grumbled in protest, but she didn't relent. "Now. Back to your dorms. Except for you five."

She made eye contact with Mia, before studying the other four. They waited while the crowd slowly dissipated. Some students moved on without question, but others lingered. They tried to stay for as long as possible, watching the gargoyles, eyes flickering over the headmistress, and the five students she had pulled aside.

Their curious expressions said they wanted to know what was going on and wanted to be the one to take the juicy gossip back to the other students. But Elmhurst had nothing but patience. She waited until the last students decided there was no subtle way for them to stay any longer, and they left dragging their feet and grumbling as they went. When they were alone, Elmhurst turned her attention to the group.

"I'm sorry, Professor," Mia said. "I really don't know how—"

Elmhurst cut Mia off. "Stop. You just saw what Mia was capable of doing. That was astonishing. I want the five of you to try her magic. Everything she has. Don't let limits on your imagination stop you. Try everything you can think of. But be careful about it. That is my only stipulation. You may try whatever you want to, but you need to be careful not to hurt others or yourselves or cause any massive structural damage to the historic buildings of the academy." She turned away, but only took a few steps before turning back to them. "And maybe you should leave manipulating the weather alone until Mia has more control. Just a suggestion."

She began to turn away again, but Mia approached her. "Professor?"

"Yes, Mia."

"Um…" The request sounded ridiculous now after the magical carte blanche they had just been given. "I'm really worried about my upcoming paper that's due on Egyptian artifact history. I want to go to the library to look up some books on the subject. I know it's late, but can I just pop in there?"

"No. It's far too late. You need to return to your dorms. But you can call up the history back in your room." Without any further explanation, Elmhurst walked away, leaving nothing but the sound of the gargoyles still cheering and laughing with glee as they flew around.

Mia could only imagine they would keep flying until their wings gave out on them. If that was possible. If they weren't really alive, maybe they never became tired. It was possible they would just fly forever.

CHAPTER EIGHT

The five hurried to the dorm. Usually, they would go their separate ways when they reached the common area, the boys to the room they shared, and the three girls into the other wing to their room.

That's not how it went that night. Instead of parting when they entered the common area, all five headed to the girls' room. Carson and Zander followed without question. It was simply understood they weren't done for the night. They may not be able to go out onto the practice field to try their usual experiments, or even attempt anything new, but that didn't mean they couldn't discuss the gargoyle's reanimation and delve deeper into the challenge presented to them by Elmhurst.

Having the guys in their dorm room was strictly against the rules, but Vivi, Luna, and Mia weren't worried about getting into trouble because of their visitors. They didn't have any other roommates or anyone to disturb, and they didn't think anyone else in the dorm would feel compelled to rat them out simply because the boys were in their room for a few hours.

Even if someone did, the chances of angering Elmhurst were slim to none. After what she experienced that night, Principal

Elmhurst seemed almost stunned. She was probably not thinking about rules and discipline at the moment. The five could get away with just about anything.

As long as it didn't hurt anyone, or involve structural damage or weather.

"That was really incredible. I mean, *really* incredible," Carson said when they entered the room. "I don't think I've ever seen anything like that."

"What? Vivi, or Mia?" Luna asked.

Carson thought about his answer for a second. At last, he gave a shrug. "I mean…both. I've never seen anyone freeze animated statues, and I've definitely never seen anyone then free those statues and let them move when they were never able to before. Do you think they could have had something to do with each other?"

"What do you mean?" Zander asked. He dropped onto Luna's bed and stared at the Unseelie boy, who reclined on a bean-bag chair in the middle of the floor.

"Think about it," Carson said. "Those gargoyles were never able to move before. They've been there literally since the library was built. And by there, I mean, right there. On those pedestals. They've never been anywhere else and have never moved other than shifting their heads around and speaking. Do you honestly think that in all the hundreds of years this place has been standing, no one else has ever had a bleeding-heart moment and tried to free them off their pedestals?"

"Hey!" Mia exclaimed. "I'm not a bleeding heart."

"Sorry. I didn't mean that in a bad way."

"Yes, you did," Vivi muttered.

"What I mean,"—Carson pressed on, talking over Vivi—"is that this couldn't have been the first time someone tried to set them free. Even if it wasn't because they cared about them. It's just one of those things. There are creatures standing there talking to you, but they can't go anywhere. Normal teenage curiosity? Someone is going to want to see if they can get them down."

"Or just to be rebellious," Luna added.

"Exactly. But they've never moved. In all this time, no one has been able to move them. Then Vivi freezes them, and they can't do anything but roll their eyes around in that creepy way." He demonstrated, rolling his eyes around for a few seconds until he realized they were staring at him. "Anyway. She can't figure out how to unfreeze them, but then, not only does Mia unfreeze them, she manages to get them totally off their pedestals and flying around. What if they couldn't have done it without each other?"

"I think you are thinking way too much about this," Zander said. "I don't think Vivi and Mia have some sort of unholy alliance we don't know about."

Carson sighed dramatically. "Mia, what do you think?"

Up until this point, Mia hadn't been paying too much attention to the conversation. Instead, she was sifting through her notes and trying to figure out how she was going to get her paper finished. She looked up at the four sets of eyes staring back at her.

"Oh. I was just thinking about..." She hesitated. "What did Elmhurst mean when she said I could call up the history in my dorm room?"

Vivi laughed and tossed herself backward onto her pillows. "So stupid," she muttered.

Apparently, all the remorse and humanity she had discovered outside the library had remained there. Vivi had already reverted to her mean-girl persona. But it didn't matter to Mia all that much. She had learned an important lesson about Vivi that night.

From the experience outside the library, Mia had learned the angry Unseelie fae girl did have a heart and a conscience. That part of her character didn't come out often, but it was there. Mia had seen it, and she had been a part of it surfacing.

She hoped she could coax that side of Vivi to come out again, and maybe eventually remain as her permanent personality. Holding out that hope meant Vivi's attitude didn't bother Mia any longer.

Dismissing Vivi's obvious need for attention, Mia turned her focus on the other three. "What did she mean?" she asked. "Is this a book-delivery situation? I can call the library and let them know what I want, and they will bring it to me? That seems a little counterintuitive. If it's too late for me to be in the library, it's too late for people to be working in there."

"It's not book delivery," Luna said. "She didn't say you could call up the books. She said you could call up the history."

Mia blinked at her. "That didn't tell me anything."

"She meant you could actually access the information and experience it." Zander offered more of an explanation.

"Not helpful."

"Look," Carson said. "You're not in your little human high school anymore. You don't have to study just by reading books or going online. The fae study in a different way. Well, some do. It takes power and skill, but we have that."

Mia rotated her hand as though recoiling a rope. "I'm going to have to ask you to go back to the beginning and pick me up there because I've missed everything that has to do with this explanation."

"You can call up images from the past," Luna explained. "You don't have to just read the words and try to get everything from that. You can actually experience what the books have to say. Like a movie. All you need is a book, and you can enchant it to spill its secrets. More information than the book even contains in print will come to life, and you can watch it."

"Do I need to remind you that I can't even enchant a storm without setting things on fire and almost drowning people?" Mia asked.

Luna laughed. "You'll be fine. We'll help you. Here, let me

show you."

The beautiful fae girl rifled through the books on the shelf against the wall and pulled one out. She lay it on the floor and spoke the words of a spell over it. A few seconds later, a glow appeared, emanating from the spine of the book. The light spread, creating a screen, where an image appeared. It reminded Mia of the few times her father convinced her to watch Star Trek with him when she was younger. Or Star Wars. One of them.

Luna had chosen a book on the rainforest, and Mia watched as an image of the jungle came to life and started moving. It was as though she was traveling through it, looking at the plants and animals around her. Every so often, the image would stop and zoom in on a specific animal or a lush plant. Words appeared beside it, providing descriptions and facts.

They all watched for a few minutes before Luna ended the enchantment and closed the book. "See?" she said. "Easy."

"Let me try." Carson scoured the bookshelf. "You have really boring books, you know that? Let me see. This one."

He pulled out a book and set it on the spot Luna's book had occupied. He opened it and performed the same enchantment. As with Luna's spell, the light appeared and created a screen.

A second later, it revealed a loud, violent battle. It was like watching a TV show about a war. It became more intense and violent, and the boys were drawn into it, engrossed by the action. After a few minutes, Luna snapped the book shut. The pages continued to glow until Carson spoke the enchantment to close the image and reluctantly tucked the book back onto the shelf.

"Ready to give it a try?" Luna asked Mia.

Mia nodded. "Sure." She picked up her textbook and opened it to an image. She followed Luna's example carefully, and after a moment, a light started glowing, and a scene appeared in front of her. It lasted only a few seconds before bursting into a ball of flame and disappearing.

"What in Hades' name was that?" asked Carson.

"I have never seen something like that happen before," Luna said.

"Me, neither," Zander added.

"Let me try again." Mia shook her head to clear her mind, flipped the page, and performed the enchantment. This image lasted a few seconds longer before also bursting into a bright fiery ball.

"I think that's probably your clue to just give up," Vivi said. "Maybe you can get into the library early in the morning."

"No. I'm not giving up that easy. I'm going to try again," Mia insisted.

This time, the fervor of her concentration resulted in the entire textbook exploding. The energy shooting from the book sent Mia tumbling backward into the wall. As she fell, she sighed, wishing she could see real artifacts and learn more about them.

In the next instant, a portal formed behind her, and she fell through.

The others didn't hesitate. One right after the next, Luna, Zander, Carson, and Vivi, dove into the portal to follow her. Mia toppled to the floor, grunting as she bounced and landed on her back.

She pulled herself up to her hands and knees and shook her head. "I seriously have to stop doing that," she muttered.

The Scooby Gang fell in a tangled heap to the floor beside her, and Mia scrambled out of the way to avoid being crushed.

"You are going to have to do some fancy explaining about why you don't have a textbook anymore," Carson said with a loud groan.

Vivi climbed to her feet and looked around. "I think she could probably find another one."

For the first time, Mia studied her surroundings. "This is definitely not what I was expecting," she murmured. "Elmhurst is not going to be amused."

They were standing inside the school's library.

CHAPTER NINE

"How?" Zander shook his head and stared at Mia. "Did *you* create that portal?"

Dazed, Mia stared wide-eyed at her friends. She tried to speak, but nothing would come out. When she winced, she also nodded.

"Did you know you could do this?" Luna whispered.

Mia bit her lower lip, not sure what she should say. Cassia and Mia had both decided to keep her portal-creation ability confidential, but now it wouldn't stay a secret much longer. Vivi would be spreading the news all over campus well before the first class started.

Other than Zander's confused look, the rest didn't seem too surprised. It was almost as though they had expected this to happen. Well, maybe not *this*, but with all of the craziness since she had arrived, the Scooby Gang had moved past immediate disbelief and into the realm of possibilities.

"I can't believe she managed to end up at the library," Vivi said with a hint of awe in her voice.

"Maybe that's exactly where she wanted to be," Luna suggested. "She did tell Elmhurst earlier that she wanted to come here and get a couple books to use while she works on her paper on Egyptian artifacts."

"Maybe *she's* in the same room with both of you, and you should talk to her rather than to each other." Mia glared at the two girls.

"You're right," Luna said. "Is this where you wanted to go?"

Mia hesitated. "I don't know."

"See?" Vivi snapped.

"How did you get here anyway? I mean, a portal, obviously, but how did you conjure it so fast?" Zander asked.

"It was the same as when I first came here. To the academy, I mean. When that happened, I was up against a wall and wished I could be somewhere safe and away from the guy coming after me. The portal showed up behind me, and I fell through."

"Yeah, quickly followed by a bullet that nearly took Zander out," Vivi added.

"Now, that's a bit of an exaggeration," Carson pointed out. "But that's still really interesting. What were you wishing for this time?"

"To be able to actually see artifacts so I can learn about them." Mia's admission sounded far more ridiculous when it came out of her mouth than it had when it was still in her brain.

"And that made the portal bring you here? To the school library?" Vivi asked. "Because it's just bursting at the seams with authentic Egyptian artifacts," she said sarcastically.

"I don't know. How am I supposed to know? And besides, where else would the portal bring me?" Mia asked.

"Uh, Egypt?" Vivi suggested.

"I want to see Egyptian artifacts, not actual Egypt. The portal probably brought me here so I could find a book on Egypt and use that to call up the information. Or have one of you call up the information so I can actually read it before it blows up."

"You're just saying that because you're afraid," Vivi accused.

"What?" Mia asked.

"You're afraid. You're afraid to try to create a portal to go to Egypt."

"I'm not afraid," Mia scoffed.

"Then do it. I dare you to try to open a portal to Egypt," Vivi said.

"This must be the most absurd conversation I have ever had. Well, no. There are a couple of other ones I've had recently that may actually rank higher. Finding out I'm a fae halfling hits right up there on the top of the list. But this one is still pretty absurd." Mia gave Vivi a sardonic look. She narrowed her eyes at Vivi. "I'm not going to try to open a portal to Egypt, and not because I'm afraid to. I have absolutely no desire to go there, no matter how good of a grade it may get me on my paper."

"How about Paris?" Luna asked.

"Yes," Vivi said the second the words were out of Luna's mouth.

"Paris?" Mia asked. "Are there a whole lot of Egyptian artifacts banging around in France?"

"Actually, yes," Luna said. "We could go to the Louvre."

"Yes," Vivi said again. She clapped her hands. "To Paris. But I don't really care about going to the Louvre with you people."

"Why would we go to the Louvre? Are a bunch of paintings going to help me any more than the books?"

"I don't think she's talking about the paintings. I think Luna is suggesting the new Egyptian display. If we get there, we could see the artifacts and the Egyptian art we need to learn about. Seeing and touching those things firsthand would give us the upper hand over the rest of the class," Zander said. "Our papers will be much better because we'll have firsthand knowledge of the artifacts."

"Pretty sure you're not allowed to touch things in the Louvre," Mia pointed out.

Carson snorted. "You can if no one notices you're there. Plus, it's the Louvre. In Paris. Do you need a reason to go?"

"So, is that a yes?" Luna asked.

"Yes!" Vivi interjected. "Yes, Paris. Yes, shopping. Oh, and the Louvre so you four can poke around old pyramid stuff." She waved at them as though she were dismissing servants.

Mia sighed. "Your resounding support is touching. All right. You talked me into it. Let's try this."

The group cheered, but they had no way of knowing they weren't the only ones in the library celebrating. A few rows away, concealed within the stacks, were Hazel and Marcus. They had hidden in the library before closing and had been there ever since, waiting to meet their vampire contact.

They would never have imagined they'd see a portal open, nor had they been prepared for the five halflings to spill out of it. They listened in on the entire conversation and were now brimming with excitement, eager to report something really juicy for once.

Mia walked around the library until she found a surface that would be good for the creation of their portal. The end of the bookshelf was smooth wood and made her feel like even if they didn't get through the portal all the way to Paris, having the surface inside the library meant they were less likely to fall out in the middle of the yard next to the building. She didn't know if that was the case, but it made her feel better thinking it.

"Right here. This is the perfect spot," she told them.

The others stood back and watched as Mia tried to conjure the portal. Nothing happened. No matter how hard she wished to be in the Louvre, it didn't work. She switched to the magic she had used with the group to create the portal, but the bookshelf remained unchanged.

Mia remembered what Elmhurst told her, and she forced herself to focus. She cleared her mind of everything around her and concentrated only on the portal she needed. She thought about the moments in the past when she had created a portal merely based on what she needed, and she directed all that focus onto the bookshelf.

And, again, nothing happened.

"What is it that you aren't doing?" Vivi asked. "You've been able to do this twice before. There has to be something you did during those times you aren't doing now."

"Are you suggesting I throw myself up against a wall and wish the portal into existence?" Mia asked.

"Couldn't hurt."

"No," Zander said. "No one is going to throw themselves against anything. I don't think this is Mia's fault. There are enchantments on the campus to prevent students from just moving around through portals however they want to. Maybe they are stopping her from being able to create a portal that sends us so far away."

The group nodded, and Mia understood now why she had portaled to the library instead of somewhere with real Egyptian artifacts. And why she had originally portaled *outside* the academy instead of inside the gates.

"But the enchantments were designed to stop the power of one fae. Let's try combining all our power together to create the portal. The enchantments might not be able to withstand that," Luna suggested.

Mia nodded. "Sounds good to me. But let's get on with it. I don't want to be lingering around here if Elmhurst decides she wants some midnight reading material."

"Uh." Vivi glanced at the ancient clock hanging on the wall near them. "It's closer to two a.m. now."

Everyone stared wide-eyed at the clock on the wall. They had been in the library for a while and had taken so much time with all of Mia's attempts and their argument over how best to create a portal that no one realized it was so late.

The five gathered together and held hands. It took a few moments for the portal to appear on the bookshelf. For all their lofty goals, it was only the size of a quarter. They all tilted their heads to look at it.

"Well," Mia said. "That's...something."

Carson leaned closer to the bookshelf and spat into the tiny portal. "I hope that makes it all the way," he said.

The girls groaned, disgusted by the Unseelie, but Zander stifled his laugh behind his hand. Mia thought about the other end of the portal. If it really was in the Louvre, someone might have just been hit with a ball of spit that came out of nowhere. Definitely not what anyone expected on a nice visit to a museum.

"We need to focus," Mia said. "There's no way we're squishing ourselves through that. It needs more power to get bigger."

They grabbed each other's hands again and took a few minutes to calm down. When they gathered all their focus, they directed their combined power at the portal. Finally, the portal began to stretch. It was almost gruesome the way it pulled, contorted, and opened. When it settled into a large enough size, they allowed themselves to relax.

"Ready?" Zander asked. He began to walk forward, but Mia stopped him.

"No. I go first." Mia released Luna and Zander's hands and entered first.

She was the one who had landed them in this situation, so she was going to be the one to test what might happen. Her hope was the portal connected to Paris, France, but for all Mia knew, it could connect to Kansas. Or to nothing.

Mia didn't think she would ever get used to traveling through a portal. She remembered the way Cassia had walked so smoothly and easily out of the portal onto the sidewalk outside the academy when they had first arrived.

It was nothing for her, as simple as walking through a door. One of these days, maybe Mia would feel that confident and go through as easily. She hoped that came sooner rather than later.

Hanging around with these four, it seemed she would likely be moving through portals pretty often.

Mia didn't realize she had her eyes squeezed shut until she hit the floor and didn't see anything around her. As she opened her eyes, the rest of the group burst out of the portal.

"You guys didn't really get the point of me going through first, did you?" she asked.

"What were you planning to do when you got through safely? Stick your head back through and yell at us?" Vivi answered.

"Carson, I think I found your spit," Luna said, her voice revealing her disgust.

Mia stood and scanned the area around them. They definitely weren't in the library anymore. The floor beneath her was made of several shades of wood, and the tall dark-red walls held ornate frames with paintings on either side of them.

"Are we really here? Did we make it? There isn't some museum wing of the academy I don't know about, is it?" Mia asked.

"This is it," Carson said. "I've been here before. I recognize this exhibit."

Vivi looked like she could barely contain herself. She was so excited they actually did it, she didn't think she could hold it in. She threw a shield up around them and squealed, jumping up and down a few times.

"What's with the shield?" Mia asked.

Vivi paused her celebration to stare at Mia. "We are in one of the most famous museums in the world. Do you know who comes to famous museums? People. A lot of them. We can't just wander around unprotected. It's essential for us to keep our gifts secret from the humans."

"That makes sense."

"Good. Can I go back to my celebration now?"

Mia swept her hand in front of her, gesturing for the other

girl to continue. Vivi jumped up and down again, and the group started talking over each other.

"I can't believe we made it," Zander said.

"I can," Mia said.

"Elmhurst did say Mia was capable of incredible things. That's enough to get through the enchantments preventing portals going off-campus," Luna said.

"With some help," Carson added.

"Well, we made it to the museum, but we're not where we needed to go. We still need to get to the Egyptian exhibit," Zander said.

"Do you know how to get there, Carson?" Mia asked.

"Absolutely. This way. Vivi, keep the shield up. We don't have the credentials to be in here, and Security might want to check our tickets."

They meandered through the different wings and exhibits of the museum and finally arrived at the entrance to the Egyptian display. Seeing it made Mia's heart jump with excitement. This was big. They hadn't simply hopped across the campus, or to a nearby area. They had gone off-campus and had traveled to a different country almost halfway around the world. It was astonishing, something young halflings shouldn't be capable of doing.

And it would help her get an awesome grade on her paper.

CHAPTER TEN

"This place is huge," Mia said as they entered the first room.

"I've never seen anything like it," Luna agreed.

"What did you think it was going to be like?" Vivi asked. "One room with a fake pyramid wall and a sarcophagus?"

"Have you ever been here, Vivi?" Zander asked.

She set her jaw, but her cheeks flushed with color at being called out. "No," she admitted matter-of-factly. "I have not."

"Then you didn't know what it was supposed to look like either, did you? So how did you expect them to know?"

Vivi crossed her arms over her chest and flipped her hair as she turned from the group and walked the few feet away the shield would allow.

"This place is enormous," Carson told them. "The Egyptian exhibit covers two floors and has dozens of rooms. It's probably the biggest place any of us have ever been."

"Then we should spread out. It's too much space to cover in a short time, and we're not going to be able to be here all day. It was late when we left the campus, and we're going to have to get some sleep before class tomorrow. Or is it today?"

Vivi thought for a moment and calculated the time difference.

If they left their library at two in the morning, it was ten a.m. in Paris. Which meant the museum was open for business. "We should just divide up and go to different areas of the exhibit, gather all the information we can, and meet back up later," she proposed.

"It would be really easy to get lost," Luna said. "It's so spread out, and only Carson has ever even been here."

"Then we should stick together," Mia suggested. "The last thing we need is for one of us to wander off and the rest of us to not be able to find them when we need to leave. I am not interested in this turning into a *From the Mixed-Up Files of Mrs. Basil E. Frankweiler* situation."

The other four stared at her blankly.

"A what?" Zander finally said.

"I guess halflings who go to fae schools don't have the same reading curriculum as human children," Mia said.

They all shook their heads.

"Let's agree to stick together," Zander said. "We'll explore the same rooms and then move on together."

They began to walk toward the first display, but Mia stopped them again. "Wait. There's one thing we haven't thought about yet. How are we going to get back to campus?"

"It will be easy," Vivi said. "We got here, so we can get home."

Mia threw her arms up in the air. "Just like that. No problem."

"Let's just start looking around," Carson said. "We can worry about getting home later."

They moved farther into the exhibit and explored the massive array of items on display. It only took a few seconds of searching to find some of the items their teacher had spoken about during the lecture.

"Look at this." Mia pointed at an elaborate necklace on a cushion under a square glass protective case. Recessed lighting illuminated the piece in surroundings darkened to protect the ancient artifacts. "Didn't the professor tell us about this necklace?"

"It looks like the right one," Luna agreed. "It's really beautiful. So much more impressive in person than it was in the picture."

She glanced up and gave a little gasp. Luna rushed to another display and pointed at a statue of an Egyptian couple holding hands in front of what appeared to be a doorway.

"She showed us a picture of this." She smiled and gazed back at the statue. "It's adorable. They look so happy."

"Really? I think they look miserable," Vivi said with a derisive snort.

"You would," Mia fired back. But guilt washed over her when a look of longing flashed across Vivi's face as she glanced at Zander. Mia tried to push on, glossing over the uncomfortable moment. "Do you see anything else?"

They continued to wander around the first room, taking in all the amazing artifacts. Several of the pieces had been in their teacher's lecture, but others were stunning surprises. Mia tried to take note of everything, wishing she had brought along a notebook and pen. She had so much to remember, and she didn't want to miss anything.

"This is really amazing," Vivi said as she moved slowly around a display pedestal with an urn taken from the burial chamber of a pyramid. "You know, any of these could be charmed or enchanted to do different things. They just look like old things dug up from tombs or found in temples. But they could actually be magical objects. It's really exciting to think about."

Luna shook her head as she joined the other girl beside the display and looked inside at the urn. "That's doubtful. Some of these items have been here in the museum for decades. Someone would have triggered the magic inside them if there was any. They wouldn't just be sitting around here without anyone noticing the enchantment."

"Like Dan and Steve?" Carson pointed out. "They've been

sitting on those pedestals outside the library for hundreds of years, and no one ever knew they could fly. *They* didn't even know they could fly. They didn't even know that they could move off their pedestals. And I daresay far more people with magical awareness and abilities have walked by those two gargoyles in the time they've been there than have come here to brush up on their Egyptian culture awareness."

Luna shrugged, apparently unconvinced. She headed over to another display within the limitations of the shield and peered in.

Mia came up beside her and examined the tiny sarcophagus. "Even still. I wish I could find something with magic. Can you imagine how awesome that would be? To find something that's just been sitting around here in the museum all this time and discover its secrets?"

"It really would," Luna replied. "Just think. Humans all think they know everything about the past. They've dug so deep into history and think they have this understanding of all the people and events from long ago. I mean, look around you. Thousands of artifacts and pieces of history from a millennia ago, and each one of them has a little note next to it explaining exactly what it is."

"Exactly what people *think* it is," Mia clarified.

"Precisely. And most of those notes are probably wrong. So many of these things had different meanings, different purposes, but those real legacies were lost with time. I don't think there's any magic left in these things because they would have been found by now, but so many of them were probably once enchanted. Humans don't even consider there being a different story behind the objects they find."

"Hey," Mia said. "Let's be a little gentler to humans. Remember, some of us thought we were human up until very recently."

Luna shook her head. "Oh, I don't mean any insult. We're all halflings, Mia. Each one of us has a human parent. I don't mean anything spiteful about humans. I'm only saying it's so interesting to see signs of our world in the context of human under-standing. They don't know what they're seeing. They have no idea the amazing potential. And even if someone told them, they wouldn't believe it."

Mia nodded. "I know I never would have. It's amazing how much my perspective of the world has changed in only a couple of months. This sounds ridiculous, but thinking about the possi-bility of any of the objects around here being enchanted makes me feel...proud. I don't know if that's exactly the right word, but to know the secrets makes me feel more connected to who I really am."

"That's lovely, and I'm honored to be here for this very special episode of 'Mia the Super Fae,' but we really need to get a move on," Vivi said. "We've only made our way through one room, and there's about a billion left to go. If we want to have any hope at all of finding everything we need for our papers, we need to keep going."

"We're not going to be able to cover enough space if we have to all stay within the shield," Carson pointed out.

"If we all agree to stay in the same room, we could probably move around without it," Mia said.

"If we all stay in the same place," Luna emphasized.

Everyone turned to stare at Vivi, who rolled her eyes. "I got it. I'll stay in the same room as everyone else. Does someone also want to put me on a leash to make sure I don't get too far away?"

"It may not be too terrible of an idea," Mia muttered.

"All right, that's enough. Vivi, put down the shield. Everybody, you have to act like you belong here, and that nothing is wrong. If you look like you are supposed to be here and are completely comfortable, you're much less likely to call attention and be ques-tioned. Stay aware of where everyone is, and we will move from place to place together. Agreed?" Zander made eye contact with each of the other four.

The others murmured their agreement and moved together

into an out-of-the-way corner of the Egyptian wing. Vivi released the shield, making them visible to everyone in the museum. It was still fairly early in the morning, and the museum had only just opened. But a handful of people were already meandering around the Egyptian exhibits. It was important to stay under the radar and not be noticed by the humans there.

If any of them had seen the five teenagers appear out of nowhere, it could have caused serious problems for them. As it was, Mia was already concerned about the possibility of security cameras catching them popping into existence from thin air. At least if the security team did witness that, the halflings had the upper hand. They would be able to disappear before security could cause any issues for them. It's not like they were likely to be seen wandering down the streets of Paris after leaving the museum.

Freed from the restraints of the shield, the group broke apart. They wandered to different parts of the exhibit, each exploring the artifacts and pieces of the collection that caught their attention the most. It gave them the opportunity to search more deeply and find the things that spoke the most to them. Mia still held out hope for finding something special among the ancient objects, to find a glimmer of magic that had gone unnoticed. They quickly lost themselves in the exploration, and time slipped by.

CHAPTER ELEVEN

It was just after two in the morning, and Hazel and Marcus were still hunkering down in the library, buzzing with excitement over what they had witnessed. They moved from behind the stacks from where they had listened to the five talk to a cluster of lower shelves near the bookshelf where the group disappeared.

Luna, Carson, Vivi, Zander, and Mia, had gone through the portal they had created only moments before, but Marcus and Hazel were filled with anticipation. They felt like they were going to burst when they finally heard a soft whooshing sound across the library.

Hazel's heart jumped, and she looked at Marcus, her eyebrows lifting, but she couldn't bring herself to say anything through the excitement.

"He's here," Marcus said, giving voice to her anticipation.

The pair hopped to their feet and rushed out into the open so the vampire they'd eagerly been awaiting would see them. They didn't want to leave him waiting or force him to look for them. He was far too powerful and impressive to be lowered to that. Finally, he turned a corner and strode toward them.

Hazel had always been curious about how José had managed to enter the school. With all of the protections put in place—he shouldn't have been able to get in, but he had. She figured someone else on campus had helped him. She and Marcus couldn't be the only ones he had forced to help him.

"Good evening, José," Hazel managed to say. It felt strange to say it since it was technically morning, but it was the only way she could think of to greet him.

"Hello, Hazel," José said. "Marcus. What do you have to report to me?"

The students exchanged glances, eager to reveal everything to him. They finally let everything spill out, from the conversation they heard, to watching the five create the portal and go to the Louvre. Their voices overlapped, and they repeated themselves a few times, but José followed along. His expression barely changed, but he nodded every now and again. A slight widening of his eyes was enough to tell them he was intrigued by the information. When they finished, both fell silent, breathless.

José thought about everything for several seconds. "Did they see you?" he asked.

Both students shook their heads adamantly.

"No," Marcus said. "We were well hidden the entire time. We only came out after they went through the portal."

"And no one else knows you were here? No one knows your connection to me?"

"No," Hazel assured him. "We haven't said a word to anyone."

He nodded again. "You've done well. Narco will be pleased. I will get in touch with him and let him know what you told me. I will be in touch when there is more to do."

José strode away from Hazel and Marcus, wanting to contact Narco as soon as possible. This information would be valuable to him, and he would want to be able to act on it quickly.

Narco had been waiting to hear the information José had

received from the two students in his service. Now his search had gone from nothing to moving fast in one conversation.

"And you are positive the girl is part of the five?" Narco asked.

"Yes," José told him. "Marcus and Hazel assured me it was the five who have been assigned to work together. They are always in each other's company, and any time they are performing any magic, it's all of them. They wouldn't be able to open the portal without her. Their magic isn't strong enough, but hers gives them what they need to be able to accomplish these feats."

"Thank you, José."

Narco ended the conversation and immediately reached out to the others in his service. He formed a team of his followers and sent them to Paris to find the group of five. He didn't care about the other four. They were inconsequential to him beyond their proximity to Mia.

It was Mia that Narco was really interested in. After watching her at the competition and monitoring her at the academy, he was becoming more confident that he had finally found the one he had dedicated himself to seeking out for so many years.

But he didn't want to act with too much haste. That had happened before, and the results were aggravating at best. Though he was certain Mia was the one he wanted, Narco needed to make absolutely sure this time. He had to confirm she truly was the girl he was seeking out, the one he wanted to destroy.

He had already killed a dozen fae girls in Faerie because he had believed they were the one. Those girls had died because he had acted far too quickly. As soon as he had a suspicion that he had found her, Narco would cut the girl down, only to discover later that he had been mistaken.

Not that the lives themselves bothered him. He felt no guilt about the people he had killed. What mattered to him was that even after those deaths, the one he was seeking was still out there. Now the bodies were stacking up, and people would notice.

With every new girl he killed, the chances of someone becoming suspicious and finding a way to link him to the deaths grew higher. He was afraid someone would find out what he was up to, and he couldn't allow that to happen. He wasn't the only one who would be interested in finding her, but the others had different motivations. Narco wanted to be the one to find her first.

If he was right this time, he had finally found the many-generations-past descendant of the long-lost third princess. Which would also mean "Mia" was not her true name. If she was the descendant of the princess, this girl would also be the daughter of the fae woman Narco had killed in Boston seventeen years ago.

At the time, Narco had believed her husband to also be fae. The man had disappeared so quickly and without a trace that Narco had been convinced he had gone to Faerie. It was the only thing that made sense. A mere human could never have outsmarted him.

That's what had led to the deaths of the dozen in Faerie. Narco had spent seventeen years searching the land to find the girl who had slipped through his fingers. He had destroyed anyone he had believed to be her. But something had changed.

He'd heard of a mysterious girl in China, a halfling who lived among humans, unaware of who she was. He had decided to check her out in case she was the one he sought. As unlikely as it seemed, he couldn't afford to let any chance pass him by; the consequences would be too dire.

If this girl was of the princess' line, despite her bloodline being as diluted as it would be by now, she could still cause serious problems for the Unseelie Court. The more he thought about it, the more he realized her having been sired by a human man did make sense.

It infuriated the fae hunter that he hadn't thought of it sooner, and he had focused his attention even more. Of course, he wasn't fully to blame. Narco might have come to the realization of Mia's parentage sooner if Flynn Terran hadn't sent him on a wild goose chase for the princess's line through the Seelie Court for the past forty years.

If Narco hadn't spent so much time searching for the descendant of the princess's line in the Seelie Court, she would never have had the opportunity to have a daughter and further extend the line.

Flynn had led him to believe the woman he sought had returned to Faerie. She was hiding there as she lived her life. It wasn't until he had killed Flynn that Narco had discovered she was on Earth. The woman he had sought was an offspring of the dead royal line, and he had finally located her in Boston. By that time, she'd borne a child. After her death, all that was left was to destroy the child, the last remaining member of the line. But the child had disappeared. Her father had whisked her away before Narco could hunt her down and kill her.

However, now Narco believed he could finally finish what he had started so long ago. He needed to confirm that Mia was the right girl, and once he did, he could kill her. He was eager to finally be done so he could stop this stupid assignment that had hung over him for so long, and move on to greener pastures. This had dominated his life for decades, and Narco was so ready to have it behind him. He was tired of chasing down ghosts and children.

Narco's team was at the Louvre, monitoring Mia's movements, but he was too on edge to wait around for them to send back any information about her. He had started this, and it would be him who would bring it to an end.

He made sure everything was properly in place here before readying himself to go to Paris. Armed with the tools he believed he may need, he opened a portal to Paris and walked through.

He arrived outside the museum, not wanting to call any unwanted attention to himself by appearing out of thin air in front of unsuspecting humans. He blended seamlessly into the groups of tourists and visitors and slipped into the museum. His magic enabled him to pass the ticket desk without paying admission, and he continued into the massive space with confidence and purpose.

Looking like he belonged was everything. People didn't question those who behaved as though they were doing exactly what they were meant to be doing. Purpose was tremendously convincing.

When he was far enough into the museum that fewer humans were watching him closely, he paused to focus on his surroundings. Calling on his tracker skills, he sought out the five students. The skill brought him to the Egyptian area of the museum and the seemingly never-ending corridors, rooms, and displays. They had already spent a few hours there, but they hadn't covered it all. He still had time.

CHAPTER TWELVE

I t didn't take long after arriving in the Egyptian section of the museum for Narco to find the five students. They were trying their best to blend in with the people wandering around the museum, and it appeared to be working for the humans around them.

Several adults moved around the students without acknowledging their presence. The five may as well be a part of the exhibit itself. The only ones who paid any attention to them at all were a few younger people who were at the museum with their parents or for school visits.

That made sense. It had nothing to do with their magic, or there being anything different about them. Like all humans, the young people were drawn by the beauty of the five halflings. Fae were astonishingly attractive to humans, and even when mixed with human parentage, their beauty shone through. The teenage humans drawn to the group of five would have no idea why.

Narco caught sight of Mia and felt a bump of excitement. Of course, it wasn't the first time he had seen her. The last time he'd been this close to her was at the slamball competition in Las Vegas. At the time, he had been less certain of her identity, but the information he had collected since made him feel more confident that he had found the one he'd been after.

Across the room, the fae bounty hunter spotted a member of the team he had sent ahead to the museum. He made eye contact with the man and acknowledged him. Narco wanted his team to know he was there. It would ensure they were ready for whatever may happen. But he didn't want to interact with them too much.

The more they interacted, the more attention would be drawn to them. He didn't want the five halflings to become aware of anyone following them through the exhibit. If they did, the quest could be ruined.

Narco slipped into the room with the halflings so he could follow them. They were gathered around a pedestal, engrossed by the vase it held.

It had taken most of the time they had spent in the first room for the sheer awe of portaling to the Louvre and the enormity of the Egyptian exhibit to lessen slightly. When it did, the five remembered they should be taking notes for their projects. Their phones coming to mind, they took them out and started snapping pictures.

After a few hours of scouring the exhibit, they had gathered an impressive assortment of photographs and stories to use for their papers. The time difference meant that in Paris, it was approaching lunchtime, but for the students, it was the very wee hours of the morning. They were all starting to feel it. Their eyelids were sagging, their bodies feeling heavier as they went from display to display.

They knew they had more information about the artifacts than they would ever be able to fit into their papers, but they didn't want to stop. Having the opportunity to be in the museum was something they knew they shouldn't have. They shouldn't have been able to create the portal or to get to this incredible place. That pushed them to keep going. None of them wanted to waste a single bit of this opportunity. They didn't want to stop until they had read all the information on Egypt and her magical past.

At the edge of one room, watching the five students exploring the exhibit in the next, Narco had reached the edge of his patience. For the last hour, he followed the group through the displays and observed their reactions to the artifacts.

At first, he'd been excited to be in such close proximity to Mia, knowing that soon he would have what he had wanted for seventeen years. But he had to bide his time, to be patient so he could confirm her identity and find just the right moment to eliminate her.

Narco was so bored that he was ready to simply kill them all and get it over with. They were wasting his time. This entire experience was wasting his time. He had believed from the beginning that a descendant of the long-lost princess would be strong and even forbidding in her power. Which was the reason she had to be removed.

Now that he was this close and watching her, every second aggravated him more. She was nothing like he thought. He had expected the royal to have skill and knowledge, but she didn't appear to have much power at all.

In fact, none of them did. From the snippets of conversations he caught as he followed them, they were intrigued by the possibility of magical artifacts tucked among the countless items in the wing. One of the girls, a lovely Seelie who seemed confident and controlled beyond her years, didn't believe such items would be in the exhibit.

The other girl, the dark-haired Unseelie who glared at the other girls with daggers in her eyes more often than not, was convinced there were. They talked about the artifacts and the excitement of what it would mean to find one. And they promptly walked right past two.

Narco couldn't believe they were so unobservant. They

should have recognized the magic contained within the two pieces. While they may have looked mundane to any of the other visitors to the museum, five students who supposedly possessed more magic and power than any halflings ever had should be able to recognize the difference.

One of the magical artifacts was a bracelet. The other was a water jug. He recognized the magic instantly but wasn't sure of its purpose. Closer inspection told Narco that if humans put water inside the jug, it would never run dry. Such a thing would be indescribably valuable for humans who often struggled to find enough clean, safe water to drink.

Mia had been feeling the creeping sensation of eyes on the back of her neck for a while. She tried to ignore it. They were in a strange place, doing something all five knew they shouldn't be doing, and becoming more tired by the minute. Which was enough to put her on edge.

But after moving through three rooms, the sensation didn't go away, and she became more concerned. Someone was watching them. Not in the curious way people tend to do when in museums and starting to blend the other visitors into the exhibits. This was pointed, purposeful watching that made her skin crawl and the hair on her arms stand on end.

She scanned the room, trying to find the person giving her the strange feeling. Three men stood out from the crowd. She had seen them in several of the other rooms the group had been through. Others had, too, of course, but something was odd about the way they moved around the exhibit.

They weren't paying attention to any of the displays. Instead, they strolled around in a very methodical, systematic way, their eyes occasionally flickering to one of the plaques or objects in front of them, but still tracking her movements. Though they didn't directly interact with each other, something about the way they moved around told her the three were connected.

Mia followed the others to the next display, separated sharply from them, and went to another corner of the room. The three men shifted their positions to keep watching her. The longer she studied them, the stronger the strange feeling they inspired got.

They didn't look like the other people visiting the museum. In fact, they didn't look all that human. It took only a short time for her to realize that was because they weren't. They were using glamours. But she could see past them and knew these three men were fae.

She returned to the group as fast as possible and moved with them around the edge of the room until they were farther from the men.

"What was that all about?" Vivi asked.

Mia gave a subtle shake of her head and guided them from the room and into the next.

"What's going on?" Zander asked. "Mia? Is something wrong?"

Mia leaned in, and the other four gathered close around her. "Did you see those three men in the other room?"

"What three men?" Luna asked.

"There are three men who have been following us through the exhibit." She glanced over her shoulder as the first man entered the room, trying to look casual. Mia tipped her head slightly toward him. "That's one of them."

Carson's attention snapped back to her. "He's fae."

Mia nodded. "So are the other two." Within seconds, the other two men filtered into the room. "There they are."

The halflings stiffened, concerned expressions crossing their faces.

"Who are they?" Vivi asked.

Mia shook her head. "I don't know. Any of you recognize them? Are they from the school?"

The thought hadn't occurred to her until that moment, but

the possibility reassured her slightly. Maybe these men were from the academy. They all knew they weren't supposed to create portals on campus, and they definitely weren't supposed to make ones that sent them off-campus. Going to a different country when they should have been in their dorms asleep for hours was totally out of the question.

It was possible that opening the portal had triggered an alarm that automatically sent the fae adults to monitor the situation and ensure they returned safely. Only, if that was the case, it would have made sense for the men to have approached them rather than merely following them.

"No," Zander said. "I don't think so."

"I don't recognize them," Carson added.

The two girls made affirming sounds, removing any hope Mia had for an easy explanation. "Whoever they are, it can't be good that they're following us," she pointed out.

"You're right," Zander agreed. "We need to get out of here."

CHAPTER THIRTEEN

Almost as though they could sense that the halflings had caught on to them, the three fae men moved closer to them. The five left the room, moving through the corridors as fast as they could without running.

"Okay, so we need to get out of here fast. Mia, can you open a portal?" Zander urged.

"I don't know. Where should we go?" Mia asked.

"Freaking anywhere but here would be good," Carson said, picking up the speed a little. The group rounded a corner and found a little space where no one could see them.

"Okay, here goes." Mia tried to focus on creating a portal. Seconds ticked by with nothing happening, and Vivi poked her head around the corner.

"They're almost here, we have to hurry!" she exclaimed.

"I'm trying," Mia said, exasperated. "It's just not worki—"

Suddenly, a dark hole appeared in front of her. It was only a couple of feet tall and so skinny they would have to turn sideways to get through it, but it was there. Without another word, Luna, Zander, and Carson jumped through.

"They're here." Vivi ran into Mia's back, pushing her and falling with her through the portal.

They landed hard on cement, and Mia batted at Vivi in frustration. "Get off of me," she said, pushing Vivi away.

"I saved your skinny butt, Mia. Those guys were right behind me," Vivi retorted.

Zander slid between them as they stood. "Hey, no time for this right now. We have to keep moving," he said.

Two girls realized he was right and nodded, and the group ran through the room. It was a long, high-ceilinged basement full of Egyptian artifacts not on display at the moment. Whether the relics were for specific displays not currently being used or they weren't deemed important enough, the halflings couldn't tell. They ducked through various aisles of items, all seemingly packed there with no rhyme or reason, when they ran past a large, ornate mirror. Everyone rushed by except for Vivi—something made her stop and call out to her friends.

"What is it?" Carson said, panting as he made it back to her. The rest of the halflings were arriving too, and in the distance, people were murmuring. The fae were in the room, and the halflings needed to hurry.

"This mirror. Look at it," Vivi said.

"It's just an old mirror—oh!" Carson noticed it too.

Soon it dawned on everyone else, and they looked at each other before turning toward the voices on their tail. The mirror showed the reflection of the room, but not of them.

Luna reached out to touch the mirror, and her hand sank into the surface. She studied the spot where her arm had disappeared. She glanced over her shoulder at the others and shoved her head into the mirror. All she saw was utter blackness, but it seemed safe.

She walked through and turned. Luna could see through the mirror to her friends as if the world was cut out of the darkness.

She poked her head back out, and everyone jumped. "Come on. It's safe!"

One by one, they each stepped through, with Zander going last. Just as he was about to follow, he heard the footsteps of the fae just beyond him. He leapt into the mirror and spun in time to see the fae man run into view.

The fae stopped, confused, and stared around him. "I swear I heard them right here," he muttered.

His gaze passed over the mirror, and everyone held their breath, but he didn't seem to notice anything about it. Instead, he turned and made a portal, which he entered and disappeared through.

Zander left the mirror first, checking the area, and waving his friends out. When the last of them were out, Luna bent to the tag on the side of the mirror and jotted the information in her notebook.

"There's another room back this way."

Carson appeared unconcerned about the details of the mirror, or his future grade. As usual, he was a bit more mission-focused. The group followed him into the next room and stopped when they saw what was inside.

"Really, Carson?" The hair rose on Vivi's arms as she stared at the figures before her. "You had to pick the room with the mummies?"

"Hey, I'm just trying to get us as far away from the fae as I can." He raised his hands almost as if in surrender, but Carson would never surrender. The smirk that accompanied his hands did nothing to settle Vivi.

Three sarcophagi were standing against the wall, their ornate carvings and decorations casting dark and ominous shadows in the dimly lit room. They towered above Vivi, and in spite of herself, she reached out to touch one. She shuddered and snatched her hand away, backpedaling until she bumped into Luna, and they both jumped.

Luna's eyes were wide and round as she stared at the sarcophagi in fascination and horror. "Someone's body is inside that thing," Luna whispered.

"Three someones' bodies are inside all three of these things," Vivi whispered in reply.

"Do you think they could be—" Luna began to ask.

"Zombies?" Vivi finished. They looked at each other and nodded slowly before focusing on the sarcophagi. There was a change in the air as panic began to take hold of them, in the absence of reason.

Mia decided to be that reason. "Zombies aren't real, though," she said. "They are made up, like in movies. It's always just a dude in liquid latex and fake blood, mumbling 'Braaiiinnnss,'" she said, rolling her eyes back in her head and holding her arms out stiffly in front of her while doing a mock shuffle-step toward them.

"Zombies are real," came a voice behind Mia. She turned to see Carson, his back pressed against the wall as he too stared at the sarcophagi. "Everything is real. Remember our talk about werewolves?"

Mia nodded, seeming thoughtful, and suddenly her eyes lit up with a combination of horror and interest. In the last few months, she had seen so many things that should fill her nightmares for the rest of her life, but for some reason coming upon yet another monster which she had believed was entirely movie magic, and finding out it was real, only made her more interested.

"So, do they eat brains? Are they brought back by a shaman? Or a virus? Or, oh, what was the other one... Right! Vampires from another planet?" she asked, going through every origin-story given to her by late-night movie marathons.

"No," Zander began, somewhat confused.

"They are rare." Carson was a little braver now that he was instructing rather than reacting. Zander might fancy himself the leader of their group, but to Carson, no one was more equipped to handle danger than him. And zombies absolutely qualified as danger. Imparting his knowledge would ensure everyone was on the same page. "They are made rarer by only being able to be revived for forty-eight hours. Then the body stops, and they go dead forever after that."

"That doesn't sound too bad," Mia said.

"Except that they can infect a human with their disease. If they do, that human can then infect other people. They can still only survive for two days, but in those two days, they can cause absolute havoc."

During Carson's explanation, Vivi had wandered off. Suddenly, her ear-splitting scream pierced the air, and everyone's heads snapped to the sound. Vivi was at the end of the room, back against the wall, holding her chest and pointing at one of the sarcophagi. The group headed toward her, but they weren't the only ones.

Nearby, Narco heard the scream too and came running.

"Vivi, it's only me," said Luna, coming around from behind the sarcophagi.

"I saw it move," Vivi shouted.

"Yeah, that was me," Luna continued, trying to calm Vivi. She glanced over her shoulder at the group for help as they approached.

"What happened?" Zander was spooked too, but more so, he was angry that Luna would take this opportunity to play a prank on Vivi. Luna usually showed more self-control than to do something like that.

"I walked around the back of the sarcophagi, just to see if it had been opened. Sometimes they are empty, you know? So I did, and I guess I must have bumped it, and it moved a little. Then —oh no."

"What?" Carson asked. "Did you break something?"

"No. Not that, look." Luna pointed out of the room and back the way they had come. A man was running toward them at full speed from way across the room, and he wasn't bothering to be quiet about it.

Mia backed up against one of the sarcophagi and sensed that the solidity of the stone wasn't there. She turned, surprised she had created a new portal. "Guys, look! I made a new portal, come on!"

They all shook their heads, confusing Mia immensely. The man was gaining on them, and though they couldn't see his face, they knew he knew they were there. They had to get out quickly.

"No way," Zander said, staring at the man before turning to Mia. Everyone else was scattering, searching for a place to hide. "A portal like that likely takes people to the Underworld. Osiris is not a being you want to be a subject of, trust me. Come on," he said, pulling her behind the sarcophagi and squeezing her close to him, so that they were tightly pushed together behind it. He wrapped his arms around her protectively as they hid. He whispered in her ear, and unlike Vivi and Luna, now was the first time the hair on her arms raised. "If we leave it active, maybe he goes into it thinking we did. Try to keep it open. Focus."

She did and held her breath as the man ran toward them. He didn't even slow down as he saw the portal and raced for it. At the last moment, as he dove in, his eyes slid across the room to Vivi, and he reached out, but it was too late. He was through.

Mia closed the portal, and they all exhaled.

Hidden only a few feet away, Narco watched, having been beaten to them by one of his own henchmen. He hid below a display of pottery and cursed silently as the group ran from the room.

CHAPTER FOURTEEN

N arco couldn't believe what he had witnessed. These halflings shouldn't be a match for his men. They should be easy pickings, ready to be snatched up the instant he gave the command.

Instead, he had watched from his hiding place as Mia led the group in tricking his man. This may be more of a challenge than he anticipated. Just because they hadn't recognized the magical artifacts didn't necessarily mean this was going to be smooth and simple. The group seemed to be able to interact with each other in a way that boosted their effectiveness.

Narco remembered what José had relayed to him from the two students at the halfling academy. The five were being heavily trained, groomed by Elmhurst to magnify their power into something extraordinary. Working together made them stronger and helped them think better.

Which meant he needed them to not be together. If Narco could separate Mia from her friends, he would be able to do with her whatever he pleased. He thought for a few seconds about how he could lure her away from them, and an idea came to him.

Following the group, he waited until the halflings entered a more isolated section and created a portal. He intended to close the portal as soon as Mia tumbled through it, but the entire group moved around it without stopping.

Aggravated, Narco chased after them. He ducked through rooms and wove through the corridors, wanting to cut off their progress. Using his tracker skills, he was able to tell the direction they were going and chose another place to create a portal. He made another, setting it into the floor so she only needed to step on the edge, and it would suck her away from the other four. Again, she avoided it and directed the others to stay away.

Frustration and anger built inside Narco as he continued to pursue the halflings. He watched them pause when Mia turned her attention to a wall in front of her. The wall shimmered slightly as though a portal was about to open, but it didn't. They were trying to escape the Louvre through a portal. Narco couldn't let that happen.

Without wasting the time to try again, Mia and the Scooby Gang raced off. Staying in one place for too long made it more likely the men would find them.

"Come on, Mia, you can do this," Zander said. "Just concentrate. You've done it before."

"I know," she said.

They turned into another corridor, and Mia saw the wall to one side begin to shimmer as a portal appeared. It spread down the wall as though chasing them, spilling onto the floor, and moving close to their feet. Mia grabbed Luna's arm and yanked her to the side.

"What is it?" Luna asked.

"Another portal. Someone's trying to trap us."

They veered around the portal and rushed into the next room. If they weren't being chased and didn't need to get out of the museum fast, she would have stopped here and spent some time exploring the incredible space. The temple room was nothing short of breathtaking.

She could almost believe they were in a true temple, taken right from a pyramid in Egypt. She wanted to stay and take it all in, but the awareness of being followed, and the threat of the strange portals appearing at their every turn, kept her feet moving.

The group ducked behind one of the massive stone pillars and waited until two women who were more invested in their whispered gossip than in the exhibit, moved out of the way.

"Together this time," Mia urged. "Come on. I can't do this myself. We need to work together to get out of here, just like we did to get here."

"We need to do this fast. We can't risk any humans seeing us do this," Vivi added.

"Back to our room, okay?" Mia said.

The rest of the group nodded and huddled together. They held hands and put as much focus as they could into creating the portal. Mia tried not to let the failed attempts weigh on her.

Finally, a portal opened in the pillar, and they sprang through without hesitation. A few seconds later, Mia landed on her face on something soft.

Having learned from experience, she rolled out of the way fast, so the others didn't crush her. She opened her eyes and realized they had landed on her bed. It was dark, but she recognized the dorm room.

Relieved and happier to see the room than she ever thought she would be, she jumped to her feet and waited for the others to right themselves. "We made it!" she gushed.

"Yeah, but we shouldn't have," Zander said.

Mia's smile disappeared, and she narrowed her eyes. "Wow. Way to just take all the zip out of the situation."

"We just had the crickets scared out of us being chased down by unidentified fae in a museum," Vivi pointed out. "I don't think there's a whole lot of zip to be had in that."

"I meant in us being able to make the portal to get back here,"

Mia snapped. "We were scared and under a lot of pressure, and we still managed to do it. We got back here. Don't you think that warrants at least a few seconds of feeling good about ourselves?"

"Maybe, but like I said, it shouldn't have happened," Zander said. "It shouldn't have worked."

"Then why did you go along with it?" Carson asked.

"Hope, fear, and the realization that we really had no other options for getting back here?" Zander said. "Unless the four of you wanted to figure out a way to hop a flight, the only way to get back to campus was going to be through a portal."

"Wait, why shouldn't it have worked?" Mia asked. "We got there through a portal."

"That was already impressive enough, but it didn't mean the reverse would be possible. It was one thing for us to be able to get a portal opened to the outside world when we were in the library. The campus already has portals in some places and the room where authorized people can create their own. They are heavily controlled, but they are there. Counteracting the security mechanisms isn't easy, but not unfathomable. But getting back into campus—that's not good."

"What do you mean?" Mia asked.

"I'm concerned we did something to damage the enchantments around campus. They may be down, or we may have created a tear in the protections put in place to guard the academy," Zander said.

"Don't worry. You didn't create a tear in the defenses."

The five gasped and jumped closer together at the sound of the voice and the sudden bright illumination when the room light flicked on. Professor Elmhurst was perched on the end of Vivi's bed, but she stood as the five turned to her. She walked toward them slowly, and Mia's anxiety increased with each measured step. She would have preferred the headmistress stalk across the room with intensity, or even run at them.

Which would have made the Elmhurst's mood more easily

readable. Her slow walk made them feel like they were being stalked, as if she was measuring them up and trying to decide exactly how severe her reaction should be.

"Professor," Zander said.

She held up a hand to silence him, her eyes closing briefly as if she didn't want to hear the sound of his voice. "Like I said, you didn't put a tear in the protections for the campus, but that is the only thing you don't have to worry about. Imagine my surprise when, after two in the morning, I heard something knocking on my bedroom window. And who do you think it could be?"

Mia knew immediately and swallowed hard. "Dan and Steve."

The headmistress nodded. "Dan and Steve. The gargoyles Mia so benevolently released from the positions they have held for centuries and who are now flying around campus, peering into windows and scaring everyone. But they didn't want to just come by for a visit. They weren't interested in showing off their flying skills or getting directions to the other buildings. No. They wanted to come by and let me know in person that an unauthorized portal opened in the library. As you could probably guess, I was pretty shocked by that news. After all, there are very specific places on campus where portals are permitted, and the library certainly isn't one of them."

Her words were as slow as her steps. There was little emotion in what she was saying, and it was unnerving.

"But I couldn't imagine why the gargoyles would make something like that up. For all their faults, they are devoted to the academy and have always wanted the best for it. So, I got dressed, and I went down to the library to examine it. There was evidence of a portal, but no one was there. Dan and Steve didn't know who did it, so we searched the campus. We checked every person, every classroom, and every dorm room. And who did we discover was missing?"

"Us," Luna murmured.

"How could you do this?" Professor Elmhurst demanded, the

anger suddenly bursting from her. "I gave you very specific instructions to return to your dorms. I told you not to go to the library, even when you asked to go to collect sources for your artifact papers. Did I not? I told you to return to your rooms and call up the information. But that wasn't good enough for you. You had to defy me and break the rules by not only leaving your room and going to the library directly against my instructions but then by creating an illegal portal. How could you do that? Do you realize how much trouble you could have caused? How much danger you could have put the entire campus in because of your stupid stunt? Zander is absolutely right. You shouldn't have been able to get back on campus. You should have been stuck. And while you didn't damage the defenses as far as we've been able to tell, you did find a loophole for getting out of campus. That is a very serious situation. And a betrayal of my trust."

CHAPTER FIFTEEN

"If I may." Carson stepped forward. It was so formal, so unlike the rest of them at this moment, all terrified and upset at Elmhurst's anger, that it actually broke the tension, causing Vivi, Luna, and Zander, to laugh.

"If you may what?" Elmhurst said through gritted teeth. She hated being interrupted, especially when she was on a good roll of lecturing, and Carson was the last of the group she expected to be cheeky. Yet, here he was, his hands behind his back, chin up and legs apart, like some TV show lawyer, ready to defend his friend against a murder charge.

"If I may have a few words, Principal. It seems like there may be a great misunderstanding that could be solved if we only took a moment, collected our thoughts, and I was able to speak on behalf of my friends."

Mia stood with her mouth gaping. She had never seen this side of Carson before, and she was taken aback. Not only was he putting himself between the group and Elmhurst, possibly incurring her wrath directly, but he was handling himself like a leader.

Not for the first time, Mia had noticed the brewing rivalry between Carson and Zander on that front, but for now, Zander was letting Carson have this chance, probably to give him enough rope to hang himself with.

Elmhurst straightened, holding her head high and stoically, with only her parted lips indicating that she, too, was taken aback. She eyed him for a moment and appeared to decide to let him talk, closing her mouth tightly so that her lips almost disappeared in a grimace. She nodded, and Carson smiled.

"Earlier when you spoke to us, you were discussing our need to push ourselves. This is a point that was very much on our minds as we proceeded through this evening," he said.

Even his voice had changed in timbre, dropping a hair lower. Either he was mimicking something he had seen on TV, or he possessed a natural inclination for the role of an attorney, but either way, his charm seemed to be working. Elmhurst hadn't expelled them yet.

Yet.

"Continue," Elmhurst said primly.

Carson cleared his throat and glanced at the group, winking as he did so. "Well, it's very simple, isn't it? You told us to try using our magic, to work together and push beyond the constraints we thought possible, as long as we didn't hurt anyone else or cause any more weather patterns to change. My question to you, Principal, is this; was there an unexpected weather anomaly this evening?"

"No." The words came out cold and judging. Carson was making a point, but he was being a jerk about it, and Elmhurst wasn't exactly enjoying the performance.

"And was anyone hurt?" Carson continued, throwing his hands to his sides as if to show off that the group stood before her, unharmed.

"Not that I know of," she said, her voice like a river of ice. It would seem safe if you didn't know how cruel and dangerous it could be.

"Then, aside from a minor infraction of the rules, this is a non-issue. Punishable by, say, a stern talking to, or at worst, an evening of detention. Certainly, considering the admittedly open-ended instructions you gave us, we are not fully to blame here."

"Oh, there is blame for you. All of you," she said.

Zander approached the principal. "Perhaps, but this is my group," he said, putting emphasis on the word 'my.' Carson fumed beside him but said nothing. "I led them during this trip, so if any punishment was to be laid down, it should be on me, not them."

"No, Zander," Mia said. "If anyone is to blame, it's me. I caused it all to happen."

"Enough," Elmhurst snapped. "If there is one of you to punish, then there would be punishment for all. Where did you go?"

"The Louvre," Luna blurted out.

She had been quiet until now, and everyone in the group spun to stare at her. She looked as surprised as they did. They hadn't discussed if they were going to be honest about where they went, but now there was no turning back. Collectively though, they all knew that certain elements of their trip needed to be kept a secret.

"The Louvre?" the principal said. "Why?"

"To gather notes on the Egyptian artifacts," Vivi offered. "Luna has a bunch of notes, don't you, Luna?"

Luna turned to her, her eyes wide and sparkling as if she didn't comprehend Vivi's words. Suddenly it dawned on Luna, and she rummaged through her bag, grabbing her cell phone.

She offered it to Elmhurst, who took it and began to flip through the images. "I also took notes in an app. We saw a lot of items that might have been fae-enchanted, and some that certainly were. It was a very illuminating trip," Luna said.

Elmhurst stared at Luna through narrowed eyes before she returned to studying the pictures. She seemed satisfied after a few images and returned the phone. Placing one finger on her lips, Elmhurst appeared to be thinking about something very deeply, and the group held their breath as they waited. Not even Carson, in his newfound confidence as the lawyer for the group, dared interrupt her.

"I want to make this absolutely clear," she said, eyeing all five of them. "What you did is in clear violation of school rules, but, as Carson so smugly pointed out, it does seem to be justified based on the instructions I, as the school principal, gave you. So, in lieu of punishment, you are all hereby on notice. Any further transgressions against the rules will be met with a harsh penalty. Do I make myself clear?"

The group nodded in relief. Even Vivi seemed pleased. Carson beamed as though he'd just won the Slamball World Championship MVP award.

"Also," Elmhurst continued. "There are to be no other portals created to anywhere on Earth, whatsoever. Do I make myself clear? Not without prior, *direct* permission to open one from me. This is non-negotiable. Are we understood?"

The group nodded.

"Good. I will see you all at breakfast," Elmhurst said, sweeping from the room.

They waited a few moments for her to get away down the hall before they burst out into celebratory cheers.

Unbeknownst to the halflings, Elmhurst hurried away with a grin spreading across her face. Mia was obviously the catalyst for the portal creation. She had been right to put Mia in the group. Now all she needed to do was help the girl to develop her powers, and her team would have no problem obtaining the Power of Five.

It was all she could do to keep from questioning them more on the *how* of it all. She'd allow them to keep their secrets, for now. But she would keep a closer eye on them when they practiced.

Her only real concern was keeping the kids safe. Elmhurst had an idea of who Mia was, but she couldn't risk researching the girl's background. Someone had chased her from China and that someone most likely knew where she was and who she was.

But if they didn't know for sure, Elmhurst wasn't going to help them out with any part of it. For now, she would help Mia become stronger and keep her safe.

Narco plugged his camera into the laptop and pressed the Okay button to initiate the transfer of the file. It wouldn't be very long now until it was fully uploaded, and he could post it to every video-streaming site he could sign up for. All anonymous, of course. Then it would simply be a matter of allowing the video of Mia opening a portal and the kids going through it to make the rounds of the school.

Once everyone saw it, Mia would be in the crosshairs of Elmhurst, which would see her expelled. Expelled meant vulnerable, and that would mean Narco could end this stupid assignment once and for all. Years of wasted time, effort, and energy would be over, and Narco could return to doing real work, not hunting down children.

It had to be her. Mia was the one. A halfling, especially one so new to her studies and her life, should not be able to open a portal at all, let alone one that took them out of the school despite all the protections the academy had in place.

Going as far as the Louvre was more impressive. The kids he had assigned to watch her had said that the portals had taken all five of the halflings to open. Yet, according to the video that was now half uploaded, Mia had opened them all on her own. And she'd been capable of closing it and creating a block so that he couldn't follow or track them at all.

It ticked him off more than a swarm of crickets on a hot summer night. To be bested by anyone, even the most powerful of fae, made him boil with rage, but for a child, a young girl who barely knew what fae were, was beyond humiliating. She was infuriating him by merely existing, and the fact that he had to resort to having other children work for him to keep her under watch, was making him wish he could simply go directly to killing her.

But that presented a problem too. She was never without someone else from her little group, and while a young, confused halfling having trouble adjusting to her new life was a much easier kill to get away with, if he killed another member of the group, the death would raise suspicion and possibly blow his cover.

Narco had to get her alone, one way or another, and excluding her from the group through embarrassment and harassment was his only way. He smiled as the video finished uploading. It wasn't as fun as getting rid of her in person, but a move like this was at least progress. One more step toward a better assignment.

The sooner he completed this age-old assignment, the sooner he could move on to something better that would help him to climb the fae social-ladder. Being stuck in this one job for so many decades had hurt his prospects, and he was done being passed over by younger and less-experienced hunters. It was time to show the world why he was the best bounty hunter the fae had ever seen.

Turning on a VPN to hide his IP address, Narco created the profiles to post under. He listed himself as a student of the academy and loaded the video. Laughter began to overtake him, and he chuckled as he posted them and copied the links to send to his spies. It would be soon now, soon the entire school would see the video and turn on her.

There would be demands for punishment, demands for her expulsion, which would make it easier for him to eliminate her. Without the protections of the academy, she was a nobody. A simple halfling who wouldn't be missed at all by anyone of importance.

The line of the long-lost princess would truly be terminated, and his assignment would be completed. He may even take a break somewhere, a vacation away from children and halflings and stupid, petty, boring, humans.

This video was the key to the beginning of her end, and now, all he had to do was sit back and wait. Narco closed the page and returned to the image of Mia. He stood and stretched, unbuttoning the top button of his shirt and removing his tie. A glass of scotch was in order for this celebration, and he pulled the bottle off a shelf.

"Salut, little one," he said, toasting the image on the screen. "I will see you soon."

CHAPTER SIXTEEN

I t was like the gargoyles had spent the entire day waiting for the very last bits of sunlight to disappear. Once she thought about it, Elmhurst realized that was exactly what the pair were doing. Now that they could get off their pedestals, all day would have become a tense waiting game for them.

They used to just sit at their posts miserably, knowing it was all they had in their entire existence. They had been crafted to sit there and had remained stuck in place for as long as the academy had stood. Hundreds of years, constantly turning seasons, merciless weather, and countless students had defined a life that hadn't truly been a life. Dan and Steve were simply animated statues with nothing else to look forward to.

Every day, all they could do was watch the students who would come close enough to the library for the gargoyles to see them and overhear gossip of what was happening on campus. Their only fulfillment and purpose had been in reporting to the professors, or to the headmistress, anything they discovered about rule-breaking or misbehavior.

Not anymore. When Mia released them, she had changed everything. It wasn't intentional. The young halfling was powerful, but there was no way for her to have known such a thing was even possible. Yet the compassion and desperate hope she had felt for the two gargoyles had somehow done what nobody had ever thought of. And in doing so, she had changed their reality forever.

Professor Elmhurst didn't know how to respond to their transformation, or what those changes meant for Dan and Steve. It was possible the effect of the release was only temporary. They could land back on their pedestals and be attached to them again. They could be free for a day, only to discover the effect gone when they tried to fly away the next night.

So far, that hadn't happened. But they weren't completely free. The gargoyles had limitations to their ability to leave their posts, and they complied without objection.

Every night, as soon as the last of the sun's rays disappeared beyond the horizon, they were released from their pedestals and free to fly around. They took to the skies and soared around campus, peering into windows and exploring hidden corners they never knew existed. But the moment the first light of morning returned to the sky, they had to be back in their places.

At first, it appeared they were merely doing what she asked and not forgetting their duty to be in their places and guard the library. But it didn't take long for Elmhurst to wonder if there was something more going on. Dan and Steve were committed to the academy, but at the same time, this was their first taste of freedom. She had expected them to remain away from their positions, at least a few times, for longer than she required them to, or even just not return one morning.

She had to admit, she was a little bit afraid they may not return from one of their adventures. She worried they would have so much fun flying around the campus that they would decide they wanted to see more, and would venture out into the world.

So, one day she asked them and was surprised to learn it

wasn't only their loyalty and their promise to her that brought them back to their positions outside the library each morning. Every night, when they took off from their spots and flew off wherever their whims took them, they knew they were on borrowed time.

As morning drew closer, the desire to go back to the library became stronger. It was an innate need, a drive to return to their places before the sun rose, and by the time the very first rays of light touched the sky, they were back on their spots where they were meant to be.

But despite that time restraint, they were happy. Neither of them expressed any real ambition of touring the world or discovering what else existed beyond the academy. They were very happy to fly around the school grounds and occasionally go a little farther into the nearby town.

They never went too far. They just flew out over the houses and peered down at the streets, enjoying all the amazing sights which neither had ever seen. Each time they flew out, Elmhurst was concerned someone would see them, and something terrible would happen to the gargoyles. But every morning, there they were, sitting on their time-honored places, watching the students, murmuring between themselves and waiting for the night to come.

That's where they were when Hazel whipped around in search of Sariah. The older girl, a senior at the academy, had spent most of the morning so far tormenting Hazel. Before breakfast, as Hazel headed toward the dining hall with a sweet, attractive boy named Lucas, Sariah had taunted and teased her about everything from her hair to her clothes. At breakfast, the older student had knocked a container of salt into Hazel's food, pretending it was an accident, though she muttered a nasty comment which only Hazel heard.

After breakfast, Sariah had made it a point to get close enough to Hazel in the hall and trip the younger girl, almost sending her toppling down the stairs. At the last moment, Lucas had run up and grabbed her arm, stopping her from falling.

He hadn't seen Sariah, and Hazel didn't mention it, but her face burned with embarrassment and anger. Going to class was her only reprieve. She didn't have to be near the older girl or wait for the next horrible thing she was going to say. Hazel hoped to make it last the rest of the day if she could manage to navigate the grounds effectively enough to stay out of her way.

Unfortunately, that break only lasted an hour. Sariah caught up with Hazel outside the library and immediately started laying into her again. No matter how hard the younger girl tried to avoid her, the senior chased after her. Sariah used a spell to make the frog-shaped brooch she wore on her sweater come to life and hop into Hazel's face. An enchantment swirled her thick hair around Hazel's head, obscuring her vision.

"Why are you doing this?" Hazel cried out. "Why can't you just leave me alone?"

"What's wrong? I thought you liked attention," Sariah snapped. "You really seem to be lapping it up when Lucas gives it to you."

"What? What are you talking about?"

From a few yards away, Mia heard the commotion and glanced up as Sariah swiped her hand angrily in the air in front of Hazel. In that instant, Hazel was lifted off her feet and flipped over, so she dangled high above Sariah.

Hazel's skirt flipped inside out and hung down to her shoulders, exposing her tights to everyone. Fortunately, they were black and thick because of the cold weather, and no one could see through them. But Mia knew Hazel would be humiliated. She raced toward the two girls.

"Don't play dumb," Sariah was saying. "You follow him around like a little puppy. Anyone within fifty feet of you can see it. Smell it, too. It's pathetic."

Now Mia knew what this was about. It was no big secret

around campus that Sariah had a huge crush on Lucas. According to Luna and Vivi, it had been going on for years. Only on Sariah's side, though. Lucas barely even knew she existed. Not so much with Hazel.

Over the last couple of months, Lucas seemed to have taken a liking to Hazel, giving her as much attention as he could. He didn't do anything over the top, but Mia had seen the way he smiled at Hazel, and he always seemed to be there to walk with her between classes or to study alongside her during breaks.

Not that Hazel took notice at all. She didn't appear to realize he was there other than to greet him or engage in normal conversations. Either she simply didn't share the attraction, or there was something else on her mind, and she was too wrapped up in it to think about him. Which drove Sariah insane. It was bad enough for the boy she liked to be interested in a younger halfling. But to have that other girl not care pushed Sariah over the edge.

Of course, Mia couldn't imagine what would happen if Hazel did notice his attention and decided to act on it. She would probably be even worse off than hanging upside down with her tights out for everyone on campus to see, her face progressively growing redder by the second.

"Sariah, stop it!" Lucas shouted, running from around the side of the library. "Why do you keep doing this?"

"Oh, Lucas, don't worry about it. I'm just playing with her. It's all in good fun. Isn't it, Hazel?" Sariah teased. The spell was holding Hazel by one ankle, and Sariah used it to yank the girl higher and bounce her around a few times.

"She obviously doesn't think it's fun," Lucas pointed out. "Just put her down."

"You want me to put her down?" There was something sinister in Sariah's voice. "You're right. She's probably been up there long enough. I wouldn't want all that information she just put in there during class to fall out of her ears. That would be a tragedy, wouldn't it?" She picked Hazel up higher. "I guess I should just put her back on the ground."

Hazel suddenly dropped a few feet, screaming as she tried to curl into a ball to protect herself when she hit the ground.

"Sariah, don't you dare!" Mia shouted as she reached them. "Don't you even think about dropping her."

Sariah made a disgusted sound and rolled her eyes, lifting Hazel up again. "You've got to be kidding me. Someone else rushing to her defense? What's with this girl?"

"Put her down," Mia commanded. "Gently."

"Why should I?" Sariah demanded.

"Because I'm telling you to. You're going to turn Hazel back over and set her on her feet. Then you're going to apologize."

Mia felt the sting of anger climbing up the back of her neck. She hated seeing the way some of the older halflings tormented the younger ones. Bullying was something she couldn't deal with. It cut too deep, and the pain lasted too long.

Vivi was already difficult enough to deal with on a regular basis. She was mean and liked to upset people, but most of her pranks were relatively harmless. She didn't go this far. Sariah was just being cruel, and Mia wasn't going to stand for it.

"Come on, Sariah. You've had your fun," Lucas said. "There's no reason to keep doing this. Just put her down and go on with your day."

Mia wanted to tell him to stop, that him defending Hazel was only making it worse. Instead, Mia moved closer and positioned herself between Lucas and Sariah. "Now, Sariah," she said.

The senior halfling merely laughed and bobbed Hazel a little more. Mia was officially done. She reached out with one hand to take control of the spell holding Hazel in the air and sent out a blast of magic with the other hand. The spell hit Sariah and flung her across the quad, where she bounced across the ground as though Mia was skipping stones. Hazel remained in the air but hung still now. Mia carefully manipulated the magic to start lowering the other girl to the ground.

Hazel tried to push her skirt back into place but was having difficulty since she was still upside down. She looked down at Mia in amazement.

"Wow," Lucas said, shocked. "That was incredible."

"I've never seen a student do something like that," Hazel told her.

"Like what?"

"You just reversed Sariah's enchantment. The only halflings I ve ever known who were able to do something like that are much older, well after college. Full fae can do it, but it takes an unbelievably strong halfling to do it." Lucas whistled and smiled up at Hazel before turning to Mia.

Mia drew in a breath and released it slowly. Add it to the list. Another thing she wasn't supposed to be able to do but had done without even realizing it.

Sweat beaded Mia's brow as she tried to maintain the magic holding Hazel in place.

CHAPTER SEVENTEEN

Before she realized what was happening, Mia began to lose control of Hazel. She was trying to maintain hold of the girl while also lowering her carefully. Mia hadn't been able to flip her back over, and now Hazel was starting to fall.

Before the poor girl's head smacked into the concrete with the force of her entire weight falling from several feet above, Cinder rushed over from her hiding place and sneezed. The spell left Hazel hanging inches above the ground, still upside-down. Mia's and Cinder's eyes met, and a smile stretched so far across the pixie's face that her cheeks hurt. Mia returned the smile as best she could despite her surprise and gave Cinder a little wave.

"Hey, uh, thanks and all, but can I get the rest of the way down now?" Hazel asked. "The blood that rushed to my head is getting rather uncomfortable."

"Oh, yeah, sorry," Mia said, and made a beckoning motion as if she was asking Hazel to come to her, and the girl spun so that she was vertical again.

"Thanks." Hazel grinned. "By the way, who are you?" Mia asked Cinder, who flashed a smile.

"Cinder," the little pixie said. "And you are quite welcome. Just glad you didn't catch on fire."

"Yeah," Mia said, and paused for a beat. "Wait, what?" She lowered Hazel to the ground.

The moment both her feet were solidly on terra firma, Hazel gathered her things, hurrying off in embarrassment.

"Bye. Thank you," she called over her shoulder, the last vowel stretching out as she ran.

"Bye." Mia waved at Hazel but didn't take her eyes off Cinder.

"That was really sweet of you," Cinder said to Mia.

"Thanks, but what in Faerie are you?" she asked so fast that both the acknowledgment and the question sounded like one multi-syllable word.

"I'm a pixie," Cinder said matter-of-factly.

"I thought pixies were a food."

"It's like a fairy. Only better."

"Oh, so like Tink!"

Cinder folded her arms, and her bottom lip protruded for a moment before she realized she had merely proved Mia's point. She thrust her arms against her sides before planting them on her hips and folded them again as she ran the gamut of stances meant to say she was upset, but she couldn't find one that didn't make her look like a cartoon.

"Cinder," she said. "Not Tink."

"Thank you for keeping her from falling on her head," Mia said, oblivious to being corrected. Somewhere in her mind, she had just stepped off a ledge and was flying above London.

"Oh, well, you're welcome."

"Want to come have some tacos? I was heading to the cafeteria, and I'd love to introduce you to everybody," Mia said.

Cinder nearly vibrated with excitement, and the light naturally emanating from her body grew momentarily in size and brightness, making Mia raise her hand to her eyes against the glare.

"I'd love to," Cinder exclaimed and zoomed around Mia's head.

"Well, come on then," Mia said and started walking away.

Over the next few days, Mia and Cinder became inseparable. Wherever Mia went, the little light of Cinder shone beside her shoulder, and the group became used to her rather easily. Except for Vivi, that is.

Vivi hated the little pixie, if for no other reason than for her immediate and close friendship with Mia. The ease with which the little imp had ingratiated herself with the rest of the group irked Vivi too. It wasn't long before Mia and Luna invited the tiny fairy to stay with the three of them in their room, which Vivi voted against, but was overruled. The pixie moved in, and Vivi was just going to have to get used to it.

Getting used to it wasn't as hard as Vivi expected, though. While on the one hand, there was always a small fire to be put out, quite literally as Cinder's magic was rather combustible, on the other hand, the pixie also tried to earn her keep by cleaning their shared space.

Once Vivi realized she would never have to clean their bathroom again if Cinder was there, she backed off on the list of pranks she had been putting together to make the pixie's life a living hell on wings. Besides, Cinder was becoming quite good at putting out her own fires, so when one happened, she was usually already on top of it. Three hundred years of practice gave her a wealth of experience with them.

Cinder wasn't the only one getting chummy with Mia, though. Much to the little pixie's irritation, Hazel started hanging around too. Knowing what she knew of Hazel, Cinder was immediately suspicious but kept her opinions to herself.

One day, Mia turned to the little pixie and asked her a question to help shed light on what Mia had been thinking. "When you look at people," Mia said as Cinder made her tiny little bed and lit a candle nearby with a sneeze that almost set the table on fire too. "Do you see colors around them?"

"Colors?" the little pixie asked. "Like an aura?"

"Yeah, like an aura."

"No." The pixie cocked her head to one side. "Do you?"

"Not with everyone." Mia dropped her voice to a fraction above a whisper. "Just with Hazel, actually. There's this glow around her, and it's a weird color. It's hard to put it into words, but Hazel strikes me as a good person, but her aura—something is off about it. It makes me uncomfortable."

"Oh?"

"Yeah. But no one else sees it. Not even you. I asked Luna and Zander, and they had no idea what I was even talking about."

Cinder kept her mouth shut, but she knew why. Halflings weren't supposed to be able to see auras. Only full fae should be able to see them. She had been arguing with herself over what to say and what not to say to Mia. If she was right, Mia was in even more danger, but there wouldn't be anything Cinder could do about it.

And if she was wrong, Mia would worry over nothing.

However, the halfling needed to know how much danger she was in. But, Cinder reminded herself that if Mia knew, she'd most likely tell her friends. She still wasn't sure Vivi could be trusted or if Carson could keep a secret this big.

No, she would continue to keep an eye out for Mia and look for more signs to tell her if the halfling was related to whom she guessed. The pixie hated keeping this from the girl who was quickly becoming her friend, but it was for Mia's safety. Cinder would simply have to keep telling herself this.

"Have you talked to any of your instructors about it?" Cinder asked, sitting on her bed. Mia dropped onto hers.

Cinder's bed was on the nightstand between Mia's and Luna's

beds, and the whiff of air from the mattress blew a gust at the pixie that almost knocked her over.

"Yes, but they didn't see it either. I asked her how she was feeling, and she said she was fine, so I thought maybe I was just seeing things."

"Or maybe it's a leftover enchantment? From Sariah?" Cinder offered.

"Maybe."

"Maybe it's something only you can see because you are the one who broke the spell? Maybe there is something lingering there Sariah has to let go of before it will disappear?"

"I don't know, but I aim to find out one way or the other," Mia said before standing. "At any rate, I need to get to class. We get our grades back today from the Egyptian Artifact papers. See you in a while."

Mia stuffed her books in her bag, slung it over her arm, and headed to class. When she arrived, the rest of her group was standing outside the door, chatting before going in.

"Mia, late again," Vivi said snidely as Mia approached.

"She's not late yet. There's still at least two minutes before the bell," Carson said. Vivi stuck her tongue out at him and folded her arms.

"Enough of that," Zander admonished.

"I still can't get over the fact we were being chased." Luna stared at Zander and Carson with a mixture of worry and hope. She hoped one of them would alleviate her fear that their safety was in question, even here in the school.

"Well, I didn't recognize them, so my guess is it was just some fae who didn't like kids using portals," said Carson.

"I don't think that was it." Zander ran his hand through his hair and looked at Mia. "Did you recognize any of them?"

"No," she responded, before falling silent. Was that accurate? "I don't know, actually. One of them looked familiar, but I didn't get a good look at him this time. It was as if I'd caught a glimpse of someone I had seen before." She shook her head. "But it wasn't the guy who went through that portal to the Underworld." Mia had wondered if it was the fae hunter who she and Cassia had seen in Shanghai. She would never forget his face. If only she could get a better look at him.

"If that's where he went," Vivi interjected. There was a moment of silence as they all envisioned the myriad horrors that would have befallen them had they not realized what it was and went through. Or if where he had ended up going was somewhere worse.

"I almost forgot to tell you guys. I did some more research on that," Luna announced. "I am pretty sure Zander was right, and that portal goes to the Underworld."

"Why?" Carson said.

"Well, the more I looked into portals attached to sarcophagi, the more I noticed there seemed to be two types: one for fae and one for humans. The one for fae would be a two-way door, and they rarely ever used them because not only could they get into the Underworld, but other things could get out. But humans only had a one-way door."

"But the thing chasing us—it was a fae," Zander said.

"True, but I think it still works like a human door regardless of who goes through. So as long as no one makes another fae portal to the Underworld they can get to, whoever it was is probably stuck there," she said.

"Man, I hope so," Carson said.

"But you said there was more than one of them down there with us," Zander said, addressing Mia. "The guy that went through the portal and someone else? Or two more people?"

"I think so," Mia said. It was hard to remember all of the details of the evening. It had all happened so fast, and she was worried maybe she had seen something that hadn't been there. Or maybe she had dreamed about it so much since then that she had added memories. Which could be why the man had looked familiar.

Only, she knew it wasn't a dream, and deep down, she knew she had really seen it. No matter how much she tried to question herself, she knew it was true. She had seen that man before, and he had been with them in the storage room of the Louvre. If he was capable of making a portal, maybe he had already let the first man out.

"I don't think we should tell anybody about the sarcophagus. The research we did on the mirror should be enough to cover any suspicion from the detail in our papers," Zander said. "If there was someone else down there with us, I suspect they would have tried to follow us, realized they couldn't and either given up or would have tried again by now, don't you think?"

There was a general murmur of agreement.

"What if they fail us because they think we cheated somehow?" Luna asked. "It's not like the mirror stuff was in any of the books we were assigned or on any of the artifacts they brought in for us to see. There's no way for us to have known about it without seeing it with our own eyes, or stumbling onto it in the Library. Don't you think that sounds pretty far-fetched?"

The bell rang above them, and Zander shrugged turning toward the open door of the classroom. "I guess we will cross that bridge if we come to it."

It turned out they had no need for concern. Just a few minutes into class, they were all beaming at each other as their papers were handed back to them with perfect scores. All five had a note from the teacher saying how impressed he was at the level of detail and of their discovery of the mirror. Thanks to Cinder, they had uncovered plenty of information about the mirror in the library to craft flawless papers. That tip had been enough for Vivi to lay off complaining about Cinder's impossibly loud snores for an entire day.

They left the classroom, gathered in the hall, and headed for the cafeteria.

"I think this calls for celebratory pizza," Carson said.

"Doesn't everything call for celebratory pizza with you?" Vivi quipped.

"Yes, but this also calls for celebratory pizza. The only problem is there's nowhere around that makes a good one," Carson said. "Why don't we open a port—"

"No," Zander, Mia, Luna and Vivi, all said in unison. The laughter that broke out was a release, but there was still tension in the air. The more Mia thought about it, the more she was sure of what she had seen, and though no one had followed them into the school, she didn't feel like they were safe yet. Something wasn't right.

CHAPTER EIGHTEEN

Thanksgiving used to be one of Mia's favorite times of the year. It didn't beat either Christmas or Halloween, which wrestled back and forth for the top spot on the list as her absolute favorite holiday, but it was a strong contender.

It ticked off all the boxes. There was beautiful fall weather that let her stuff herself into stretch pants and her favorite sweatshirts and sweaters. There was an abundance of amazing smells, from the burning leaves outside to the spices and food inside. There was time with her father, and watching favorite movies all night. There was a week of leftovers they had said they would turn into all sorts of interesting and innovative foods, which they had ended up eating directly from the containers.

At least, that's what the holiday used to be for her. Not this year. Mia was going to have to get accustomed to her new normal as a fae halfling at the Elmhurst Academy, and that meant looking ahead to a day without any of those boxes ticked. Starting with the fall weather.

Back home, there would be the possibility of some flurries, maybe a dusting of snow on the local foothills, but for the most part, she would get to enjoy the last of the year's pretty leaves and crisp, clean air. Getting up early wasn't her favorite thing, but during the fall, she made it more appealing by wrapping up in her much-loved blanket and standing out on the porch with a steaming cup of coffee or hot tea.

It was going to take a whole lot more than her threadbare pink chenille blanket to ward off the cold, and the winds, of the Montana Thanksgiving. The end of the previous week had brought a massive snowfall, and the snow had kept piling up over the following two days until the students were trapped by several feet. From the window of their dorm, it looked like they were stuck in a huge snow globe, which someone kept jiggling.

Not that it made a huge difference to many of the students. For the most part, the academy closed down for the Thanksgiving holiday. The majority of the students went home to celebrate with their human families, and to enjoy some time away from campus and all their academic pressures as finals loomed before Christmas.

Mia knew that wasn't going to be her. As much as she missed her father and wished she was in her favorite sweatpants awaiting her first heaped plate of mashed potatoes, stuffing, and green bean casserole, she wasn't going to be seeing him this year. As far as he was aware, she was still in Shanghai, learning under a master and wouldn't be able to make the trip back to the United States for the holiday.

Mia imagined this would hurt his feelings and knew he missed her, but her father would also be so proud of her. Seeing her excel in her martial arts meant a lot to him, and he would willingly give up that time with her if it meant she was able to pursue her dream. Part of her wondered if he would be as proud, knowing where she was and what she was studying. She hoped he would be.

Carson dropped onto the wooden bench of the table in the dining hall beside Mia. He crossed his arms on the table, sighed, and dropped his head onto them. It was a dramatic display, but one she had seen from Zander the day before, so she knew what it meant. "Your parents?" she asked.

He nodded and lifted his head. "They called to wish me a Happy Thanksgiving."

"But they aren't having you come home?" Mia finished for him.

"Nope," he said.

He dropped his head onto his arms again, and Mia rubbed his back to comfort him. The five were all sitting around the table, none of them sprung from the academy for the holiday by their parents. Both Carson and Zander had received calls from their human parents, but neither was summoned home, which had disappointed both of them.

"Did you think any of us were going to get out of here?" Vivi reached into the basket in front of her and pulled out a biscuit.

"You make it sound like prison," Mia said.

Vivi shrugged and scanned the dining hall. "It's starting to feel like it. Even if our parents had called us out for the holiday, I doubt Elmhurst would have let us go. She's kept us back for every other break."

"She didn't say she was going to do that this time," Carson pointed out.

"Does it make any difference?" Vivi snapped. "We're all stuck here."

The Unseelie halfling was taking staying at the school over Thanksgiving the hardest. That surprised Mia. Vivi's human parent was her mother, and since she had died, Vivi had no human connections.

Full fae didn't celebrate Thanksgiving. It was purely an American human holiday, which meant fae had no reason to see the break as special in any way. Vivi's father would be living his normal life, working every moment, and would see no point in complicating things by having his daughter home, just for the sake of a break from school.

The only one who didn't seem deflated by the thought of spending Thanksgiving at the academy was Luna. Considering it was only her and her mother, and her mother was human, they always celebrated Thanksgiving. And since she was close by, Luna didn't need to leave school in order to visit her. Staying on campus was easier. But that didn't mean she wasn't going to help the others enjoy their holiday as well.

"Come on, guys. I know you're disappointed about having to be here, but the holiday isn't ruined. We can still celebrate Thanksgiving," she chirped.

"Is your mom making dinner again this year?" Zander asked. His voice held a little bit of a lift as he asked the question, as though the thought may make the week easier.

"Of course, she is."

"What dinner?" Mia asked.

Luna turned to her with a smile. "There are always some students left at the academy over Thanksgiving, and my mother can't stand the thought of people being alone for holidays. Even fae who don't celebrate it. So she started a tradition of hosting a huge Thanksgiving dinner at the diner for the students who didn't leave the academy. It's all vegan, complete with tofurkey and all the trimmings. Anything you can think of for a traditional Thanksgiving dinner, she makes it. It's a really wonderful night. I hope you'll come."

"Absolutely. I will," Mia said. "Thank you. I was having a hard time thinking about celebrating this holiday without my father, but it will definitely be easier if I can spend it with you guys."

"I just hope the snow lets up by then," Zander said. "It would be hard to get to the diner with it like this."

"I'm sure it will," Mia said.

She was wrong. They woke up Thanksgiving morning to a fresh three inches of snow on top of what had already fallen. Luna was in the dining hall before the others arrived, staring at the table and looking disappointed.

Mia sat across from her. "Good morning," she said. "Happy Thanksgiving."

Luna looked up at her with sadness in her eyes. "It should be. But with this snow, how are we possibly going to get to the diner to have dinner? I'm not going to be able to see my mother for the holiday, and we're not going to get to eat all the amazing food together." She sighed and looked at the table again.

"That's not necessarily true," Mia offered. "There's another way we can get there."

"What do you mean?" she asked.

"I know what she means," Carson said from across the table. Their eyes met, and she gave a little nod.

"So do I," someone said from behind Mia.

Mia turned to find Principal Elmhurst standing close behind her. "Oh. Good morning, Professor. Happy Thanksgiving."

"Happy Thanksgiving to you, too, Mia. I hope you aren't talking about making a portal to go to the diner."

"Honestly, I was considering it," Mia admitted.

"You know you can't do that. We've been over this. You are not permitted to make any portals that take you off-campus to anywhere on Earth. That includes Nicolette's diner," Elmhurst said.

"But it's the perfect solution," Mia argued. "I've already proven I can make a safe and reliable portal. And those brought me a whole lot farther than just into town to the diner. But I don't have to be the one to do it. You could open a portal for us in the secure room so you would know exactly where it was and where it would get us. It would be the easiest way to get us all there safely and on time for dinner. We wouldn't have to deal with the snow on the way there or on the way back, either."

"Yes, Mia. I could open a portal very easily, and it would be a fast way to get everyone directly to the diner." The five young halflings grinned at each other, but Elmhurst shot down their growing happiness by shaking her head. "But I'm not going to do that. Luna's mother has several human workers, and there may be human customers at the diner today. There's no way we can risk having them see us coming through a portal. It would be disastrous. I'm very sorry, but a portal is just not an option."

Luna sagged against the table again. "So, dinner is out."

"I didn't say that. We can still get there. It will just take some organization and a little bit of adjustment. But I'll take care of that."

Luna grinned, and Mia's heart soared. It may not be what Mia was used to, but she was going to get Thanksgiving, and she was excited about it.

That afternoon, a bus appeared in front of the school, with another one right behind it. All bundled-up, the students shuffled down the snowy steps and into the cushioned seats inside, eager for the dinner that awaited them.

For many of them, this was a rare and unusual treat. Most students who stayed behind at the academy during Thanksgiving were like Vivi. They only had contact with their fae parent, and so they didn't celebrate the holiday. Several had never celebrated it until Luna's mother started throwing the dinner when Luna entered the academy. Despite not having a full grasp of what the holiday meant, or why they were celebrating, the fae students loved the spread of delicious food and the fun of all being together.

When the students were all on board, Mia noticed Elmhurst walk up to the front wheels of the first bus and say something while sweeping her hand over the tire. She repeated the process on the other front tire and moved on to do the same for both front tires of the other bus. When she returned, the headmistress flashed a smile at the students.

"That will take care of the snow for us," she said.

"What was it?" Mia asked.

"Just a little bit of magic. I can't do anything that will drastically change the snow, or the humans will notice. But that enchantment will pack the snow down just enough to make it safe and easy for the buses to get through on the way there and back," Elmhurst answered.

When they arrived at the diner, platters of food had already filled several tables Nicollette had pushed together and draped with a crisp white cloth. Candles burned along the center of the table, and though the place-settings were the dishes used by the diner every day, they managed to look elegant. Luna ran to hug her mother, and several of the students followed suit, thanking the smiling woman for all she did for them.

Warmth spread through Mia's chest as Nicollette hugged her and welcomed her to the dinner. It felt like the holiday should. They sat and started passing the platters and bowls around, filling their plates with the vast array of dishes prepared for them.

They dug in, and for the next half hour, the diner was filled with the sound of chewing, glasses clinking, and dozens of conversations bubbling among the halflings. When everyone had eaten at least one round of food, Nicollette stood at the end of the table and clinked a knife against a glass. Everyone looked up at her, and she smiled, raising her glass to them.

"Happy Thanksgiving, everyone. I am so glad you were able to join me for the holiday. I'd like to further our holiday celebration by going around the table and sharing what we each are thankful for."

They went around the table, and Mia smiled as she listened to each of the students talk about the things in their lives they were thankful for. A few students giggled, but for the most part, it was a heartwarming way to find out more about each other. Just listening to them share these little glimpses into their minds made her feel closer to them, even though she hadn't met some of them before that day.

When her turn came up, Mia looked around the table, and at her group spread out on either side of her. So many emotions churned through her that she didn't know where to start describing them. But she did know exactly how thankful she was and what was making her feel that way.

"I haven't been a part of Elmhurst Academy as long as the rest of you. I haven't been a part of this world as long as the rest of you have. But it's been an amazing journey. I've learned so much about myself and my history and what I can become. Not just about being a halfling, but about me as a person. I know there is no way that would have happened if it wasn't for the people who have brought me—sometimes kicking and screaming—this far. They were asked to do this, whether they liked it or not. And the 'or not' was a good portion of the time, I know. But they were there anyway. That's why I want to say that this year, I am thankful for all the friends I've made at Elmhurst Academy. Including you, Vivi."

Vivi's gaze snapped to Mia, and her mouth fell open. She blinked a few times, processing what she had just heard. Mia opened her arms and pulled Vivi into a hug. As Mia squeezed her close, Vivi sniffled, fighting back tears.

"No one has ever been thankful for me before," Vivi whispered.

"I am," Mia whispered in reply. She didn't know if it would change anything, but she was glad for the moment she had shared with the Unseelie girl.

"I know we're thankful for you, Mia."

Mia turned to the door of the diner, where Steve and Dan were standing. Gasping, she stared around the restaurant, worried the gargoyles would be seen by the humans.

"Don't worry," Elmhurst said from the head of the table. "When they told me they were planning on coming as soon as they were released from their pedestals at sunset, I made some preparations. Nicollette sent the human staff home early, and once the human diners who were here left, I put up a block to prevent any others from coming."

"We wanted to be a part of your holiday celebration," Dan said.

"It's the first time we've gotten a chance to do anything for Thanksgiving other than watch people leave," Steve told Mia.

"Well, I'm happy to see both of you," Mia replied. She crossed the diner and gave each statue a kiss on the cheek.

The crowd spent nearly two more hours in the diner, finishing their dinner and tucking into massive sweet-potato pies, pumpkin pies, and chocolate cakes. When they were all finished and sufficiently stuffed, they piled into the buses to head back to the academy. Dan and Steve soared high above them but didn't return to the library. As the five went to the dorm, the gargoyles followed close behind.

"What are you going to do now?" Dan asked before they went inside.

Mia turned to them. "We were thinking about watching some movies. Maybe playing some games."

"Mom sent me back with lots of leftovers, so as soon as we have room, we'll eat some more," Luna said.

Mia smiled at the gargoyles as they exchanged glances. "Do you want to join us?"

Dan grinned. He seemed a little star-struck by Mia, while Steve maintained some distance. Even with his reticence, he appeared reluctant to end the evening there, eager to spend more time with the students.

"Sure!" Dan finally agreed.

The gargoyles entered the dorm for the first time and followed the five halflings to the girls' room. The guys left but returned a few minutes later, having changed into their sweats. The girls took turns going into the bathroom to change, and soon they were all comfortable and ready for a night of hanging out and enjoying the holiday together.

They stayed up all night playing board games and cards, watching movies, sharing stories, and eating their way through as many of the leftovers as they could stuff inside themselves. They didn't even think about going to bed until the gargoyles announced they needed to leave so they could return to their spots in time for the sun to go up.

Dan watched as Mia crawled under her covers and rested her head on the pillow. She sighed as her eyes closed, and he felt more secure leaving. Ever since they had gained their freedom, they had been watching over Mia more closely but hadn't noticed anything out of the ordinary.

They truly enjoyed their time away from the library, and they wanted to make sure the time they spent did some good in addition to being fun. For now, Mia seemed safe and content, so the gargoyles slipped out of the window and returned to the library. They touched down on their pedestals with mere seconds to spare before the first bits of sunlight came across the sky.

CHAPTER NINETEEN

The weekend after Thanksgiving was going to be insane this year, and Vivi was ready for it. Starting on Sunday, the slamball championships was to be held over three full days of late-November mayhem, and since the Halfling Academy was hosting this year, there were no classes the entire week.

Even though it meant the students were drafted via random lottery to perform various tasks, like helping with parking, janitorial duties, ushering, and concessions, it was worth it to get the break from class and experience the insanity of all the different academies descending on Montana to liven the place up.

Vivi had yet to be assigned any duties and was more excited than she otherwise would have been at the prospect of being able to enjoy the games without any responsibilities, unlike the others. Luna and Carson had both been drafted into ushering for the heads of the academies, and Zander and Mia were assigned cleanup duties.

Vivi might be assigned to work one of the refreshments stands or some other job, but for the moment, she was free, and she felt like rubbing it in everyone's faces while she still could.

This included Amanda and Uri, two Unseelie girls she used to hang out with.

Amanda and Uri were as inseparable as two peas in a pod. Though they came from very different cultures, the two of them had bonded immediately at the academy and were known for their loyalty to their little clique of friends, which at least theoretically included Vivi. Both were wearing the blue-and-gold aprons assigned to the cleanup crew, and Vivi was dying to tease them about it.

"Hey ladies," Vivi said as she approached them. "If I spill my drink everywhere, can I ask specifically for you two to come clean it up, or is it random?"

"Very funny," Uri said as she turned to her, away from whatever deep conversation the two of them were giggling through before Vivi arrived. "What did you end up with?"

"Nothing. I get to watch the games and throw my trash on the ground and go back to the dorm to watch TV while you push a broom around."

"Unless you get drafted for bathroom duty," Amanda said, a smirk crossing her tiny, scrunched-up face. Vivi thought she looked like a constipated chihuahua.

"Yuck. Don't even put that out into the world, Amanda," Vivi said.

"Why don't you ask her?" Amanda said to Uri, who stared back, eyes wide, and shook her head sharply. "Come on, it would be great."

"Ask me what?" Vivi said, suddenly intrigued.

"Fine," Uri said begrudgingly. "We have this plan, and we want to know if you think it's vicious enough. We're on cleanup crew with Zander and, ugh, *Mia*." She said Mia's name as if it physically pained her. "And we were going to do something really cool."

"It's so great," Amanda butted in. "We're going to build this big mess of trash, and then when she goes to clean it up, I'm going to enchant the mustard bottles while Uri goes behind the refreshment counter and—"

"Absolutely not," Vivi said, leaving both of them with their jaws open, though Amanda's was still bouncing up and down a bit.

"Why in the Underworld not?" Uri demanded.

"Look, she may be weird, and she may not really belong here, but..." Vivi closed her eyes as she tried to force the words to come out. She nearly lost the battle. "But she is my friend. Crickets, I can't believe I said that. It's true, though, and if anyone is going to mess with her, it will be me. If I catch wind of either of you doing anything to her, you'll catch it back tenfold from me. Got it?"

"Yeah," Uri said, straightening and holding her hand out to Amanda, who took it. "We got it. See ya around, Vivi."

Vivi waited until they went around a corner before she kicked the wall, hard. What the heck was she doing? On what planet did she stand up for Mia, of all people? She was leaning against the wall when she happened to notice the clock.

Only a few hours remained before the big orientation in the auditorium, and she wanted to get dressed for the occasion. When she arrived at her room, her heart sank. A note was taped to the door, with the official stamp of the academy on the front and her name written across it in the scrawling print of none other than Elmhurst.

Vivi, I noticed you were not yet assigned a duty for the championships. We are low on both bathroom attendants and assistants for the VIP's. Considering your recent grades, and the impressive way you have handled the changes to your team, I have chosen to give you the VIP assistant duty. Do not make me regret it.

-Elmhurst

Vivi smiled so wide it nearly split her face in two. Having the week off would have been nice, but being able to sit in the VIP section and only worry about fetching drinks on occasion? That was worth bragging about.

As they walked out to the fields together, the group shared the details of their various duties and times. Thankfully, they all had the first couple of matches off and planned on sitting together to watch them.

Mia gasped as they approached the soccer fields, which had been enclosed using some fairly powerful magic to create two large stadiums. The covering shimmered in the sunlight, and while it was possible to see through, it was impenetrable by weather—an incredibly strong version of the domes the group created to practice in.

"This is incredible," Mia said as they entered the first stadium via a portal arranged specifically for the games.

"It's really cool. I'd love to know who is casting the spell, but they keep it a pretty closely guarded secret, for obvious reasons," Zander said.

"It has to be at least one representative from each school, though, all working together. We know that," Carson said.

"Why?" Mia asked.

"So that if one of them decides to sabotage the games because their team is losing, the others can hold it together and hold that person accountable," Luna informed her.

"So, there are four people, then?" Mia asked.

"Eight," Vivi interjected. "One for each team participating."

"Wait, I thought there were only eight teams total, two from each elite academy? Is everyone in the playoffs?" Mia asked.

"No, that's just our league. Our league is the Premier League, where the elite schools have A and B teams. There is another league for the other levels of academies. Overall, there are a total of fifteen academies in the US and Canada, and they participate in two leagues. The Premier League and the Banner League. The Banner League is older, and consists of all the original schools from before the Elite schools were created. Most of the lower academies come from the Banner League and end up placing fifth through eighth and filling out the playoffs, and the rest end their season," Luna explained.

"There is only one elite school for each species; Fae, Shifter, Vampire, and Witches. Obviously, we are the Fae Academy, and each elite school has an A and B team. Does that make sense?" Zander asked.

Mia nodded, and she tried to work it out as they entered the lower concourse of the stadium. The magic was more than merely the dome over the fields, it was also enchanting large sections of seating around the grounds, climbing high and angling in.

Each section of seating, lower, upper, and VIP, was separated not by concrete but by magic. They floated in place, and the VIP seating actually moved, driven by a spellcaster in each pod of seats to go where the VIP's told them to. Occasionally, one would dip down between two lower concourse seating areas, and fly back above the playing field to get a better viewing angle as the casters showed the guests all the positions possible for the day's game.

The grounds itself was covered in its own protective, though almost invisible, dome. While the shield over the fields shimmered in the sun and snow, the dome over the stadium was ethereal and intangible. It was as though it were made of the thinnest of smoke, and you could only see it if you screwed up your eyes just right, like attempting to look through the holes in a fence made of gossamer.

They climbed to their seats, up in the nosebleed section, via a complicated portal-to-stairs system. They found their places near the front. Once settled in, Mia figured she could learn a little more about what exactly was going on without feeling like a complete moron, but to her disappointment, Vivi sat between her and Zander, and Carson was on the other side between her and Luna. If she was going to find anything out, it was going to be through the wide eyes and excitable temperament of Carson, or the cutting sarcasm and dismissive attitude of Vivi.

"I know the championships are played out over three days, but I am still a little confused as to how it works," she said, loudly enough in Zander's direction that she hoped he would hear over the crowd and the loud music blaring through the arena.

Instead, Vivi turned, and to Mia's surprise, didn't look at her as if she had just asked if she could eat soup with a knife. "It's a series of brackets," Vivi said, raising her voice over the noise as they began to perform a stomping-and-clapping routine to music that was a well-known slamball tradition. "Our A team made it in as the second-place team, so we play the seventh-ranked team first. That's Shilo Academy, one of the lower shifter academies from Sonoma County, California. We played them last year, but we were third place, and they were sixth, and they stayed in it to the last few minutes. It was embarrassing, but we finally won. We got knocked out by the Shifters' Premier League team in the semi-finals, and people say it was because our team was so shaken by how hard it was to beat the Shilo Shifters."

"But they were in second to last place this year, and we were second place, so it should be an easier game, right?" Mia said.

This time it was Carson who chimed in mid-stomp-and-clap. "If we don't do better this year, heads are going to roll. Their main gunner graduated last year, and they've been spectacularly bad all season. They only placed seventh because their schedule was almost all B level teams. Even those games they barely won. We should mop the floor with them."

"Remember last year, though," Vivi said, and Carson grimaced.

"I don't want to," he said.

"Our A team is actually the favorite to win the championship this year," Vivi continued. "We only lost one game, and that's to the first-place team, the witches' A team. There was a lot of weird stuff happening in that game, and one of the referees was placed on suspension, but nobody knows why. The rumor is that one of the teachers paid them off to call fouls on us, but no one will say. We are on the opposite side of the bracket as them, so if we can make the finals, it will likely be against them. It's really rare for any of the non-elite teams to make the final four, and the witches are likely to sweep their bracket."

"Then we get revenge," Carson said. He sipped a drink Mia wasn't sure she had seen him buy, and they stood for the playing of the Fae Academy Anthem. The game was about to begin.

CHAPTER TWENTY

"Do you mind if I sit with you guys?" came a voice from behind them, and Mia turned to Hazel, who held a tray of nachos and her ticket, with an expression of hopeful hesitation on her face.

"Yeah, come on," Mia said, and beside her, Cinder muttered something under her breath, but no one else heard it.

The seats were general admission in the upper decks, and the group reluctantly scooted closer together to create the space for Hazel. She was rather small anyway, so it wasn't much room, but it did make everything a little tighter, and it put more space between Mia and Vivi. Though Vivi had been acting a little better recently, keeping a bit of distance was probably a good idea, as far as Mia thought.

Unfortunately for Hazel, Vivi wasn't a fan, and she rolled her eyes and made a face when Hazel sat, as though she had been forced to smell Carson's gym socks.

Sitting between Vivi and Mia wasn't exactly Hazel's preferred scenario, and despite Zander moving over a fair bit, Vivi barely scooted to give her space. She squeezed in anyway. "So, do you have a favorite on the team?" Hazel said as she wiggled into the spot, looking from Mia to Vivi.

"No," Vivi said curtly.

"I'm still really new to the sport," Mia explained. "So, I really don't know much. I think the gunner position is cool, but I don't know any of the players or anything like that."

"The team captain is pretty dreamy." Hazel sighed. It took both Vivi and Mia aback, and they glanced at each other, trying to suppress a laugh.

"Dreamy?" Vivi asked snidely.

"Thorison Granger. He's really, really good," Hazel continued, as Vivi rolled her eyes again.

"You should know," Carson muttered, and Mia shot a questioning look at him. "What? Her dad is a former pro-player. Now he's the academy scout."

"Is that true?" Mia asked, twisting to look at her new friend, who went red in the cheeks and appeared shocked to be called out so bluntly.

"Yes," she said. "He is. I guess I see more of the players than most people do because of it."

"How much more?" Vivi leered, and it took a second for Hazel to understand the implication.

"Not *that* much," she exclaimed as the meaning dawned on her, and a bubble of giggles built into full laughter and rolled through the entire group. Eventually, even Hazel laughed.

As far as the gang was concerned, having Hazel around could be useful, if for nothing else other than her family connections, but to Mia, she was something more. She seemed nice, and aside from her gang chosen to be her friends, Hazel seemed like someone she might organically be friends with, and it meant a lot to her to have someone like that. Besides, Hazel was younger and small, and it felt good to have a little-sister type person after the journey to get to the academy left her feeling like *she* was the little sister.

"It's really coming down out there," Zander said, looking up. The dome's roof was mostly transparent, and when they took their eyes off the field of play, where the game was beginning, a look around showed the grounds of the school being absolutely hammered by snow. It piled up in great drifts and blew around so thick it was difficult to see more than a few feet beyond the protection of the dome. Even the tall, imposing spires of the school were mostly covered by the snow. Silently, Mia thanked every deity imaginable for the portals that would get them where they needed to go.

Luna had explained to her earlier that during times of major snowfall, Elmhurst created portals that took the students from one building to another, so they didn't have to walk in a blizzard. These were semi-permanent pathways that were closed when not needed.

Mia hoped it would give her more of an opportunity to learn how to better use them without making a fool of herself each time. If she kept falling through the portals, she was never going to feel like she belonged.

The game was mostly uneventful, and as the buzzer finally sounded, the score was lopsided in favor of the Fae Academy. The Archers, the A team, dominated the entire game and even played the last few minutes with bench players.

Many in the crowd left early, but the gang stayed back until the very end, Carson munching on various snacks. Eventually, Hazel said her goodbyes and left the group, who sat in the nose-bleeds chatting away. The next game was going to be in an hour or so, so they had a little time before they had to leave.

"I know what we should do," Cinder said, interrupting an argument about trampoline vs. hovering-flight strategy between Luna and Zander. "We should have a bonfire!"

"During a blizzard? Are you nuts?" Vivi asked.

"Seriously? You guys can create a shield big enough for all of us to stay safe from the storm and have the bonfire inside, dum-dum."

Vivi's face ran through a range of emotions, beginning with shock and rolling through indignation and into anger rather quickly. "Listen here you little fleck of fairy light, I could—"

"All right, all right," Zander said, interrupting Vivi. "Enough of that. I actually agree with Cinder."

"What?" Carson and Vivi reacted with varying degrees of disbelief. Carson's words were rather garbled by the number of chocolate candies in his mouth at that moment.

"It could be a good test for Mia, actually. To see if she can create a shield on her own and hold it. It's something all of us can do, and it's important she gets it right because you never know when you will need it."

"That's fair," Carson eventually agreed. "But if we are going to have a bonfire, we are going to need something to roast over it."

"S'mores," Cinder said. "You guys bring the s'mores stuff, and I'll bring the fire. I'm really good at fire." She laughed at herself as the group got the joke and joined in.

"It's agreed then," Zander said. "We can use portals to get back to our rooms and fetch supplies and then use the portal to get back here and just do the bonfire right outside the dome. Come on, let's get going."

Zipping to the dorms, Zander and Carson grabbed the graham crackers, a favorite of both boys, while Luna dug into her stash of chocolate, and Vivi and Mia searched for marshmallows. It ended with both girls sneaking down to the empty kitchens and nicking the first bag they saw.

"You think anyone will notice?" Mia asked as they ran giggling to their room.

"Nah, not with the games. Come on, I need a coat. I still don't trust you not to turn us into snowmen."

Mia shook her head and laughed off the mild insult. For once, Vivi seemed to be having fun *with* Mia and not *at* her. Besides,

Vivi was probably right. They had at least a fifty-fifty shot of all being buried in several feet of snow.

Mia tried to calm her nerves about it with the excitement of the upcoming s'more feast, but it lurked in the corner of her mind until they reached the portal and walked through, into the safe area outside the two stadiums. That's when the nerves went into overdrive.

"I don't know if this is a great idea," Mia said slowly. "What if I get it wrong and somehow ruin the games or something?"

"Don't flatter yourself," Vivi said. "The domes over each stadium and the big one we're in right now are impenetrable. It's fortified with the magic of eight leaders of the various academies, and they have backup-security protecting it beyond that. The stadiums will be fine. I'm far more worried about turning into a popsicle."

"She's going to do fine." Zander smiled at Mia. "Let's get out there."

Following his lead, the group of five, plus Cinder, safely tucked inside Mia's coat to prevent her from blowing away, exited the protection of the main bubble. The cold hit them instantly, and they rushed to a section of the courtyard where they could build a fire and turned to Mia. There was no going back now.

"Mia, you have to do it now," Luna shouted over the sound of snow pelting them.

The blizzard-like conditions were disorienting, and the snow seemed to be piling up as Mia watched it. They already had to take giant, high steps to move, and in only a few more hours, the snow was bound to be over their heads.

Mia tried to focus, closing her eyes and holding her palms out to her sides. It was a position she had seen Vivi and Luna take, and they both said it helped them, while Zander and Carson said it made them look like weird statues. Mia figured she would rather resemble a statue than fail, so she put herself in position and focused on the idea of a dome around them.

The wind seemed to settle, and the snow wasn't falling as hard. Mia smiled as she thought of how impressive it would be to have built the dome on the first try, and the heat from the sudden bonfire, wood collected by Carson and Zander with fire provided by Cinder, began to warm her skin. She raised her hands higher and opened her eyes.

Suddenly she wasn't in control anymore. Her smile faltered. The dome, purple-hazed and pulsing like a living being, had swallowed them and seemed to thin. Holes began to open around it in various places, including one in the center above the fire. A large block of snow fell in and landed on the wood, extinguishing the flames.

There was a moment of absolute silence as the dome disappeared, and they all stared at the snow mound that was once a fire.

Luna started laughing first. Then Zander. Then Vivi. Finally, Carson joined in, despite the stick he held out, the marshmallow long lost in the white snow. Soon enough, Mia began to laugh too.

"All right, so that didn't work. Try it again, before we all freeze to death," Zander said.

At that moment, the two gargoyles landed heavily on either side of the group. Dan stood tall, sniffed the wind, and stuck out a stone tongue to catch some of the fluffy flakes falling from above.

"You should poke holes in your dome," Dan said. "So the smoke can escape. You can't see it, but even the ones over the stadium have some holes poked in, just on the sides."

"But with fire," Steve interrupted. "You will need your holes at the top because the smoke needs to escape. A little bit of snow getting inside won't hurt you."

"They're right," Luna offered. "Give it another shot, Mia."

Mia closed her eyes again and tried to focus, letting the concept of the small holes at the top swirl in her mind. She felt it begin to form, and the wind and snow slowed down. Soon, it felt warmer again as the fire sparked to life once more. Slowly, she opened one eye and stared around her.

The smoke was rising to the top of her dome and escaping through tiny holes. The fire roared in front of them and was so warm Carson was taking off his coat. Marshmallows on sticks were being passed around, and the gargoyles looked on in smug satisfaction before flying off to wherever it was they felt like going for the evening.

The group spent an hour roasting marshmallows and making s'mores, chatting about the night's win and their predictions for the bracket of teams. Mia listened with interest, but something was bugging her. The snow was piling up at the top of the dome, and she was worried that when she released it, it would dump on them all. She couldn't create a portal either, so she needed to figure out another way to move the snow first.

Various ideas were running through her head when something caught her eye. Just outside the dome, between them in the courtyard and the shield covering the soccer fields and makeshift magic stadiums, someone stood in the snow and watched them. His eyes were piercing and menacing, and he was looking into their dome with great excitement.

Only he wasn't looking at the group, or the fire, or the s'mores. Not even at Cinder, the magic fairy who zipped around, creating more sparks when the fire grew low. His eyes were locked on Mia's. And she remembered where she had seen him before. *Twice* before.

First in China at her Wushu competition, then in Paris. She hadn't been sure it was Narco since she didn't get a good look at him, but now she knew it had to be him. He was the one who had chased them through the Louvre. Just before someone else ended up in the Underworld. Her eyes were locked on Narco.

CHAPTER TWENTY-ONE

The sight of the fae standing right outside the dome made Mia's skin crawl and her stomach flip. Fear tingled along the back of her neck and made her breath catch in her chest as she remembered barely escaping from him in the museum. That had been one of the most terrifying experiences of her life.

In many ways, it was more frightening than the day she had to run from the monsters chasing her moments before she had tumbled through the portal and landed at the academy. Perhaps more than that, she hadn't understood then what was chasing her. The reality of who and what she was hadn't sunk in, and she hadn't known the full extent of the world she belonged to. She didn't know enough to be terrified.

But now, she did. She knew the dangerous fae with cold eyes posed an incredible danger for her. Finding them in the museum wasn't a fluke. It wasn't the first time he had come after her. Of course, the first time, she hadn't understood what she was seeing, or that he had any connection to her at the time. She still didn't understand why he was chasing her. But with him only a few feet away from her now, this time, the fae's presence made her feel sick.

Mia pushed away the fear, replacing it with defiance and anger. He had no right to make her feel that way, no right to threaten her and her friends. Especially here. The academy was where they were meant to feel safe and secure. Coming this close to them was going too far.

She had to do something. She refused to let him get to any of the others, or to her. Some of her fear seeped through her anger, but she held strong to the resistance and turned it into a sense of strength and focus. She glanced at Zander, catching his eye and gesturing with hers toward the menacing fae.

He stiffened when he saw the man from the museum and gave her a knowing nod. The look traveled to Carson and to Vivi, finally reaching Luna. They all knew he was there and what his presence meant.

"I'm going to go ahead and remove the shield now," Mia announced, trying not to reveal in her voice any of the edgy emotions she felt. "Is everybody ready?"

The students all agreed and braced themselves for the snow to come in on them. Mia knew they didn't need to prepare. At least, she hoped they didn't. She had something else in mind. Bringing all her focus in again, she cleared her mind, centered herself, and concentrated on her plan.

On either side of her, the group lined up, creating a wall between the academy and the hunter. Mia sent a blast of magic to the dome, at the same instant disintegrating the shield and forcing the snow away from her as hard as she could.

Just as she hoped, the pile of snow that had collected on the top of the dome, sped toward the tall fae. Before he had a chance to move out of the way, it dumped down on him. The heavy white snow buried him, concealing him within the mound. Mia didn't allow herself even a second of relief.

"Go!" she shouted to the others. "Get to the school."

Knowing the fae bounty hunter was digging himself out and wouldn't be held under the snow for long, they raced to the school. They had to get away as fast as they could, to be as far from the spot as possible before he got out so he couldn't catch up with them.

Not everyone left. Steve and Dan stayed where they were, watching the mound of snow. They wanted to monitor the stalker's progress and know when he freed himself. The students needed to be out of the way, but someone had to know when he escaped the snow.

They couldn't just let him roam free without anyone knowing where he was. The gargoyles had no reason to fear him. Even so, the sight of him made them uncomfortable and angry.

That also gave them the pleasure of seeing him scramble his way out of the snow, which was great fun in itself. They glided low to the ground, wanting to keep their feet out of the snow as they watched.

It took a while, but finally, his hands emerged from the top of the mound, pushing and clamoring in the snow until he could pull the rest of his body out. Soaking wet, with clumps of snow clinging to him, the fae looked comical and infuriated at the same time. He didn't notice Dan and Steve watching.

He had been seen, and he had no time to waste. He had to escape. He had paid a great sum of money to guarantee a way in and out of the campus, and now was not the time to be caught. He could return again as long as his secret passage was kept secret. Furious and frustrated, he ran toward the trees, scanning the area to ensure no one had seen him leave.

Dan and Steve watched the fae leave the campus grounds, and as soon as he was outside, he created a portal. In an instant, he was gone. The gargoyles returned to the school as fast as they could, heading directly for the headmistress.

The group of five halflings was already in her office when the gargoyles reached the window and peered inside. Mia spotted them and gestured until Elmhurst opened the window and let them in.

"Did you see him, Dan, Steve? Did you see the fae watching our kids?" the headmistress asked when they flew inside.

The gargoyles nodded.

"Yes," Dan said. "We watched him escape from the snow. He left the grounds and used a portal to leave."

Professor Elmhurst thought for a second before rushing to her desk. She reached into her drawer, pulling out what appeared to be a small, parchment-bound book. As she flipped it open, she glanced at the gargoyles.

"Dan, Steve, I need you to do something for me."

"What do you need?" Steve asked.

Both were poised to help, ready to do whatever they could for the headmistress, and for the five halflings.

"Fly around campus and gather up the professors. Get all of the staff. Direct them to the meeting hall. Make sure they understand it is of the gravest of importance. Tell any students you see to go to their dorms and wait there until a professor comes to speak with them," she told them. "Please, hurry."

"Yes, Professor," Dan said.

"Right away," Steve added.

They burst from the window and soared off across campus. Both felt a tremendous sense of purpose and drive. They had spent their entire existence at the library, wishing they could have some impact, that they could actually do something.

Spying on the students and passing along information to any adult who happened by was the most they were ever able to accomplish. It wasn't much, and it rarely had any real effect. Now, they had their chance. It was finally time to truly serve the academy they loved.

"What are you going to do, Professor?" Mia asked.

"If he came onto the campus once, he will do it again. Only next time, he'll be better prepared. He won't want to be denied again. The academy needs to be protected. I'm going to put the school on warning. From now until Christmas break, the campus will be under strict control. Student movements will be limited to the dining hall and the dorms. Unnecessary extra-curricular activities are suspended until further notice."

"But Professor Elmhurst. The championship!" Carson argued.

Zander shifted uncomfortably, not wanting to say anything, his expression strained.

"Yes, Carson. The Championship will continue. The other schools have come to Elmhurst for the games, and we're not going to disappoint them. With additional security, we will continue with the competition as planned."

"Additional security?" Luna asked.

Elmhurst studied the book again. "I'm also going to call in extra full-fae adults to act as additional guards for the campus. Mia, that includes Cassia."

"Cassia?" Mia asked, stunned to hear her guardian's name. It had been a long time since she had seen her, and Mia was surprised to learn that the headmistress held her in such high regard that she would reach out in such dire circumstances.

"Yes. She has been keeping up with you from a distance, monitoring your progress here among the other halflings. She hasn't wanted to interfere. I've been keeping her informed. As a precaution, I reached out to several fae to be ready to come and guard the school if needed. She joined that number after the incident at the museum. She volunteered to come whenever I need her," Elmhurst told her.

"Does she know? I mean, will she..." Mia was not sure what she was trying to ask. She hated the idea of putting Cassia at risk but was also confident that the strong, powerful woman could hold her own.

"She is one of our best bounty hunters. She won't have any trouble protecting herself, or you."

Mia nodded. "When will she get here?"

"I'll reach out to her today. I don't know when she'll be able to come, but hopefully, it will be soon. I want the academy protected as soon as possible."

Mia went to bed that night with a sense of foreboding pressing in around her. The other girls fell asleep more easily, but she lay awake, listening for the occasional sound of Dan and Steve peeking into the window to check on her.

And Carson and Zander were right outside. They had moved their bedding into the hallway and were camping there to be ready if something happened. It was reassuring to know they were there, but at the same time, she wished they would return to their own room. If they did, it would be more normal, and she wouldn't have to feel as on edge.

The next morning, Elmhurst came to the room, moments after the sun rose. Mia heard the boys groaning, their blankets moving across the floor before the door opened. She was already up and dressed, having given up sleeping almost an hour before.

"Mia, Cassia is here," the headmistress announced.

Mia rushed to follow her out of the dorm and across campus back to her office. As soon as she arrived, Cassia ran to meet her and gathered her into a tight hug. "Are you all right?" she asked.

Mia nodded. "I'm fine. Really."

Cassia forced a laugh through her worry. "Adding that 'really' makes me not believe you. You know that, right?"

Mia laughed. "I'm glad you're here."

"I am, too. I wish it wasn't for this reason, but I've missed you. I'm glad I could come. I want to know how everything has been going," Cassia said.

"Go down to the dining hall for breakfast," Elmhurst told them. "I'll be gathering the whole school together later this morning to introduce the additional guards and announce the rules."

Cassia and Mia sat beside each other at one of the long tables at the dining hall and dove into plates overflowing with French toast dripping with maple syrup, fruit salad, roasted potatoes, and plant-based bacon. Hot cups of coffee continuously refilled themselves as long as they drank. They would do so until either the fae or the halfling no longer wanted any, then the cups would drain. It was a favorite feature of the school for Mia, who found not having to get up for a refill an unimaginable luxury.

"I've been keeping up with you through the headmistress," Cassia said to Mia. "But I want to hear from your perspective how things are going."

Mia nodded as she pulled apart a piece of bacon and swirled it in a pool of maple syrup on her plate. "It's actually going really well. Most of it, anyway," she said.

"Most of it?" Cassia asked.

"Yeah. I just...I mean, I guess I thought a halfling academy would be less—"

"Like your old high school?" her guardian asked.

Mia chuckled. "Exactly. I guess I figured since it was full of a bunch of other people who didn't exactly fit in, there would be more of a sense of unity and less bullying."

"Not so much, huh?"

"Not so much." They laughed together. "It's not too bad. I can handle it."

"And the other four?" Cassia asked. "How is the Power of Five coming?"

"We're working on it constantly. We've accomplished some pretty amazing things. At least, I think they're amazing. But I still think everything's amazing. However, other students and even teachers have told us that the things we're able to do are a big deal."

"That's fantastic. I'm so proud of you."

Mia smiled. "Thanks."

"Your father would be really proud of you, too."

Mia's head dropped slightly. "I miss him."

"I know you do," Cassia told her. "I knew it wasn't going to be easy for you to be here and not be able to see him. But you know it's for the best."

"I do understand that, of course. But it still doesn't make it easier. Especially with the holidays. Thanksgiving was hard enough, and it was really nice. We all got together and went to the diner, where Luna's mother had made us a wonderful meal. Then we just hung out for the night. It was almost like being with family."

"They *are* your family," Cassia said, but Mia shook her head.

"No, they're not. Not really."

"Well, I'd like to think I'm part of your family. At least in a way. So I think you should come home with me for Christmas."

Mia's eyes lit up, and her heart lifted. "Really?"

"Absolutely."

"What do you look so happy about?" Vivi asked as the other four halflings came into the dining hall and joined them at their table.

"Cassia just invited me to join her for Christmas," Mia told her.

"That's wonderful," Luna said.

"It can't be for the whole break," Cassia said cautiously. "I would have to bring you back here December twenty-sixth. I'll have to go back to work, and I can't take you with me."

"Oh." Mia shrugged. "That's all right. It's better than having to stay here on campus by myself for the holidays."

"Why don't you come home with me after that?" Luna asked. "You can come stay with me and my mom through the New Year. It would be fun."

"Do you think that's all right?" Mia asked Cassia.

"That's a really sweet offer, Luna. Mia, I'll give you permission to stay with her, but only if Elmhurst says it's safe for you, and for Luna. Now…" Cassia sat taller in her chair and looked each of the five in the eyes. "Tell me everything you know about this fae who's been trailing you. I want to know what he looks like, everywhere you think you've seen him, and what exactly he's been doing."

For the next forty-five minutes, they discussed the mysterious fae and what they have all noticed so far.

Cassia grimaced. "Are you sure it's Narco? Is there any video of the guy?"

The five glanced at each other and shrugged.

"Wait." Luna put a finger up. "The Louvre. It might have video of him. Whoever posted those videos of us online had to have been the fae who's been following us, right? And most likely, he's on camera as well."

"Great idea. I'll look into the video myself and see if I can confirm his identity. I do know most of the bad guys, after all." Cassia laughed, but it wasn't a joyful sound. She was worried about who it might be. And if it was Narco, she knew Mia was in real danger.

Despite the lingering darkness on the edge of her consciousness, the tension building on campus as the new rules locked things down, and the new guards appearing, Mia was beginning to feel happy again.

CHAPTER TWENTY-TWO

M ia didn't know if she could handle the tension. Anxiety coursed through her. Cold sweat coated her palms, and her shirt was damp and clammy against her skin under her coat. Her pulse pounded in her temples, and she could barely hear anything else around her other than the rush of the blood in her ears.

The feeling kept building, stronger and stronger until she thought she might pass out from not being able to breathe. Beside her, Luna appeared pale and slightly dizzy. She didn't even look at Carson on her other side. His reaction would be just as intense. But she couldn't do anything other than wait.

Finally, it happened. The buzzer splintered the air, and all the tension broke into screams and cheers. Mia jumped to her feet and threw her arms in the air, laughing and hopping up and down. She turned to Luna, who shrieked and grabbed her up in a tight hug. They'd done it. Elmhurst Academy had won the slamball championship.

Sheer delight filled Mia as the stands around her erupted in a celebration so deafening, she didn't hear Zander's voice behind her. But she felt his hands on her shoulders, and when she looked up at him, he was grinning and saying something.

Everyone was beyond thrilled, buzzing with excitement over the exhilarating final game of the competition. It had come right down to the last seconds, the schools of both teams sitting on the very edges of their seats as they waited for the last points to be scored and the final buzzer to determine the champions.

Now the air around them sparkled with green, gold, and silver confetti, enchanted by one of the teachers to fall endlessly from the ceiling. The confetti disappeared as soon as it reached the ground, creating a never-ending cascade of shimmer around the students.

What made it all the better was that nothing had gone wrong. There had been no other threats, no sign of the bad guy, or any of his men since he had left through the portal. The extra fae guards had monitored the campus, and the rules stayed in place to keep the students safe, but everything had remained calm throughout the rest of the competition.

Even the students from the visiting schools had fallen into the pattern of the new rules, and it didn't seem to change their daily life too much. Being required to go from the dorms to meals, to approved activities, and back to their dorms, had also forced them to spend more time together. So, in a lot of ways, the restrictions strengthened friendships and gave students time to get to know each other better.

Not that Mia ever forgot what was going on. She had never pushed the mysterious fae, or his mission, out of her head. He was always lurking there in the corner of her mind, hovering at the edges of her thoughts. Seeing Cassia every day was wonderful, but it was also a reminder of the trouble. If Mia wasn't in danger, her guardian wouldn't be nearby. And part of Mia was always on guard, ready to act if she needed to.

But today she was setting her worries aside and allowing herself to be excited. With as involved as she had ended up becoming in the slamball competition, she felt like she had followed the game her entire life. Though she had only recently learned about it and started watching, she was definitely a fan now.

Sometimes, after watching a game, she would toy with the idea of taking up the sport herself. It had been so long since she had practiced her Wushu—which used to take up most of her life —that she missed having something to devote herself to that way. Her magic was different.

Her power was something she had been born with that she merely needed to rediscover and develop, like an advanced form of walking. Practicing and mastering a sport was different, and the thrill of competition never grew old.

Of course, she would never ever share those thoughts with the others. Mia couldn't risk Vivi hearing it during one of her bouts of sour mood and turning it into yet another opportunity to taunt and humiliate her. Things were definitely better between the two girls since Thanksgiving, and for the most part, Vivi was still standing up for her and being as friendly as Vivi was capable of being. But a few flickers of the bristly Unseelie girl still remained.

Mia didn't have any time or energy to actually pursue anything other than her magic. If she had, she would have been at least trying to maintain her Wushu skills. At least until everything was settled, and they had achieved the Power of Five, she was simply going to have to channel her overachieving, competitive spirit into honing her fae abilities.

Today, though, was all about enjoying the rush of the win and celebrating with her friends. Soon the semester would be over, and they would all break for the holidays. The visiting schools would leave, and everything would settle back into their normal routine. She wanted to savor as much of the fun before that as she possibly could.

"That was amazing!" Carson exclaimed as they bounded down

the stands and out into the crowd. "Did you see that final play? I had no idea which way it was going to go."

"Seriously. That was bordering on miraculous. I've never seen playing like that," Zander agreed.

"It must be something in the snow," Mia said. "It's all just *magical.*"

She did a happy twirl, but Vivi only glared at her.

"You do realize you're in Montana. It's *always* snowing in the winter in Montana. Of everything on this campus, the frozen crystals that never stop falling are the least magical thing," she said.

Mia couldn't help herself. She tilted her head in Vivi's direction and stuck her tongue out at her playfully. To Vivi's credit, she smiled.

Luna linked arms with Mia and Zander, looking at both with a wide grin.

"So, what are we going to do now? We have to do something," she said. "We have to celebrate!" Carson agreed. "We should have a party!"

"I think that sounds like a fantastic idea."

The five turned to Elmhurst, who stood behind them, smiling wider than they had seen since the first time they were able to combine their magic successfully. A few pieces of confetti sparkled in her hair, and she held an Elmhurst Academy pennant in one hand.

"Really? Awesome! Mia, you can make a dome like last time. Where's Cinder?" Carson started looking around for the little pixie, but Elmhurst rested a hand on his shoulder to stop him.

"Like I said, a party sounds like a fantastic idea. But let's give Mia a break this time. I'll have the teachers create the party dome for us." She paused and leaned a little closer as though sharing a secret with the five. "And we'll see what they can conjure up."

The halflings exchanged glances and grinned. A surprise was coming their way. Elmhurst told them to join the other students for lunch, and they would find out later what was up her sleeve. The five hurried to the dining hall, excited to talk more about the thrilling win and to wait for Elmhurst's big reveal.

They managed all the way through lunch, spent an hour afterward lingering in the dining hall talking with the other students, and another hour in the common area of the dorm working their way through a board game they'd been trying to finish for more than a week.

They gave up on the game because they couldn't concentrate, and decided to go outside and talk to Steve and Dan. As much as all but Mia hadn't expected they would feel this way, they all found themselves missing the gargoyles during the daylight hours. The group had become so used to spending time with them as soon as the sun had set that now it seemed strange and quiet when they weren't there. It made knowing they were stuck on the pedestals even sadder.

Though that day, it might have been good for them.

"I didn't know they had to sleep," Mia said, staring up at the statues.

"I didn't, either," Carson said.

Both gargoyles stood in their usual positions on the pedestals, but their heads were hanging, and their eyes were closed. If she didn't know they couldn't die, Mia would have been extremely worried about them. Suddenly, Steve cut loose a jagged snore as Dan released a whistling exhale.

"I don't think they really *need* to, necessarily," Luna said. "It's more like they've gotten into the habit of it. Remember, they've never been able to move before. Maybe now that they can fly, they get tired."

"I wouldn't think their stamina would be very good after a few centuries of not moving more than turning their heads," Zander pointed out. "They've been doing really well, considering."

"Look!" Vivi exclaimed.

Mia turned to the Unseelie girl, who was pointing excitedly toward the fields at the back of the school. Her voice was loud enough to disturb the gargoyles, and Dan lifted his head.

"What's going on?" he asked, his voice groggy.

"She's doing it!" Vivi said. "Elmhurst is setting up a party."

"What kind of party?" Steve asked.

It almost sounded like he was still asleep, muttering something in a dream.

"I guess you two sleepyheads haven't heard yet," Mia said. "Elmhurst Academy won the slamball championship!"

"Yeah, and we suggested there should be a celebration, so Elmhurst is setting up a party," Carson said.

"She's doing that just because you suggested it?" Dan asked.

"Well, probably mostly because if she didn't, we were going to have Mia set up another dome," Carson said.

"Ah. She wants to cut down on her liability."

Mia gasped as though offended, but she knew the gargoyle was kidding. "You should come to the party when it's set up," she said. "Celebrate with us."

"Maybe we will," Dan said.

Which meant that they would. His aloof act wasn't fooling her. Waving at the statues, the five halflings rushed to the field to watch the progress of the party setup. The headmistress looked at them as if she wanted to scold them for not waiting for the announcement, but she was also excited. She and a number of the other teachers moved around a dome several times larger than the one Mia had made right after Thanksgiving.

It was much more impressive than hers, not only in size but also in the fact it wasn't overflowing with snow. Instead, it expelled the snow off the top and threw it so it fell several yards away from the edges of the dome. Inside, the adults conjured games and carnival rides, and the smell of fair foods wafted toward them.

"Almost ready," Elmhurst promised them. "Just a few more finishing touches to go."

CHAPTER TWENTY-THREE

The party was like nothing any of them could have imagined. Even if the five halflings had tried to come up with what they thought Principal Elmhurst and the other teachers would create for them to celebrate the win, their ideas would have fallen far short of what they saw when they finally got to go inside.

It felt like it took forever for them to finish setting up the party. The five halflings roamed around the outer edge of the massive dome, watching everything the teachers were conjuring, thanks to the ingenuity of Zander. As they walked, he *moved* the snow out of their way, giving them enough space to stroll comfortably along the dome.

It seemed that when they noticed what they were sure was going to be the most amazing detail, something across the space would catch their attention, and they went running to see that instead. The result was not being sure of everything inside, and being excited to finally get a chance to explore.

In the last few minutes of their preparation, the teachers enchanted the dome to go from absolutely clear to bright shades of blue, red, purple, green, and gold. It almost resembled a circus tent, and the new opaque quality meant they didn't get to see everything going on inside. Elmhurst's voice boomed out around the campus, amplified by her magic. She invited everyone to come down to the field and enjoy the celebration. Mia and the other halflings were the first in line at what they assumed would be the entrance and, oblivious to the cold, waited eagerly for the grand reveal.

They were excited when the swarm of students came through the academy portals to join them. It wasn't only students from Elmhurst. Many of the kids from the visiting schools had decided to stay a little longer and joined them as well. It created an even more exciting atmosphere that turned from merely a celebration of the Elmhurst win to a unifying celebration of their entire time together.

The groundskeepers were working overtime to push the snow back to make room for all of the students to stand outside the circus dome. Mia watched in wonder as the snow flowed backward in an arcing waterfall, taking the white puffy bits of frozen water away from them and farther out toward the trees. Though the snow was still falling, at least it wasn't covering their legs while they waited.

Instead, the snow barely touched the ground before it was whisked away in a magical wonderland.

The horizon was starting to tint with the colors of sunset when Elmhurst finally appeared at the edge of the dome and came through it to talk to them. She grinned broadly and held out her arms, presenting the dome. Mia expected some big speech similar to the one's teachers were so prone to make in any situation they thought could be a teaching moment.

Instead, she just said one word. "Enjoy!"

The entrance to the dome appeared, and the colors of the sides faded away to reveal the carnival inside. Everyone rushed forward and spread out to cover the huge space inside the dome and discover all the surprises waiting for them. The five ran directly for the Ferris wheel in the center of the dome.

Instead of the usual plain buckets to ride in, this wheel had cars shaped like various creatures and vehicles. The first one that came around resembled an enormous old-fashioned hot-air balloon. The girls hopped into it, and the ride operator closed the door behind them.

As they rose into the air, the two boys climbed into the next bucket, which was shaped like a dancing elephant. The one behind that was a miniaturized version of a locomotive with a whale and a tiny pirate ship across the center of the wheel.

"I'm trying to figure out the theme of this Ferris Wheel," Mia said with a laugh.

Luna and Vivi studied the wheel.

"Well," Luna said. "Looks to me like the theme ended up being a bunch of adult fae with their own ideas, and it exploded into nonsense."

"That is the most perfect party theme I've ever heard of," Mia said.

"Hey, look. There's Hazel." Vivi pointed over the side of the hot-air balloon.

Mia turned from where she was leaning against the side and looked down at the young halfling. Hazel didn't seem to be as wrapped up in the fun of the party as everyone else. Instead, she wandered aimlessly, looking around and watching others walk by.

Marcus came up to her and muttered something that made Hazel's face go dark. The hot-air balloon was climbing higher up on the wheel, making it harder to see what was happening between them, but her posture appeared defensive. She began to move away, but Marcus grabbed her arm.

"What's going on there?" Mia asked.

Luna shook her head. "I don't know, but it doesn't look pleasant."

Hazel pulled away from him, and they exchanged a few more words before another boy approached. Mia realized it was Lucas. He moved partway between Marcus and Hazel and held up a hand to Marcus.

"Looks like Lucas has it all settled." Vivi had a hint of mischief in her voice.

"I hope Sariah doesn't see," Luna said. "The last thing we need is more of that."

"Hopefully, even Sariah wouldn't want to ruin the party by acting like that again," Mia said.

"And if she does, you'll set her straight, huh?" Luna said, nudging Mia playfully.

"If I have to."

Below them, Lucas said something to Hazel, and the pair walked across the dome.

"Where are they going?" Vivi asked, turning around to watch them as their hot air balloon reached the top of the wheel.

"Feeling nosy today, Vivi?" Luna asked.

"Just curious," Vivi said.

She leaned far over the side of the balloon. "They're getting cotton candy."

The guys laughed at the report.

"So scandalous!" Carson yelled.

Vivi leaned farther, and Mia's heart jumped into her throat. She grabbed Vivi by the back of her shirt to tug her into the basket.

"What are you doing?" Vivi asked, shaking free of Mia's grip.

"You were going to fall," Mia said. "I was just stopping you."

Vivi snorted. "Are you serious? Elmhurst and the teachers made this thing. Do you really think they'd let it be dangerous?"

When Mia didn't know what to say, Vivi shot her a teasing look and swung her leg over the side of the basket. Mia gasped as the other girl dropped out of sight. She rushed to the edge and looked over, only to see the Unseelie halfling floating a few inches below. Vivi hovered there for a few seconds, grabbed hold of the edge and climbed back in.

"What was that all about?" Mia asked.

"Halfling baby-proofing," Carson yelled between cupped hands over his mouth.

"They just want to make sure the students don't get hurt," Luna told her. "Whenever there is something like this, they put safeguards in place to stop any of us from ending up injured. Not that there has ever been anything quite like this before. But once we did have a zip-line and somebody unhooked their harness."

"Somebody being Carson?" Mia asked.

"Well," Carson replied, sounding extra huffy. "I'd be offended if it wasn't the truth."

"How is Carson hearing all of our conversations?" Mia squinted at the boys in their own ride. It wasn't far from them, but it shouldn't have been close enough for him to listen to everything they said. Especially since he had to yell back at them in order for them to hear him.

Carson's face split with a joyful grin. "Magic, my dear. Magic." He flitted his hands in the air like a human magician, and a colorful scarf flew from his fingers.

Luna giggled. "He's got this spell he likes to use for eavesdropping. He can hear us as though he's right here with us, but we can't hear him."

Mia nodded. "Huh, not a very good spell if he had to yell for us to hear him."

"Hey, I heard that," Carson shouted. "I'm still working out the kinks."

They all enjoyed a laugh. Mia narrowed her eyes and tilted her head. "If the teachers can just make it so you can't fall like that, why bother to have the buckets for the Ferris Wheel at all? Why not just have the teachers float you around in circles for a while?" she asked.

Vivi rolled her eyes and stared out over the party again. "See, that is how everybody knows you were raised among the humans," Vivi pointed out.

They laughed and spent the remainder of the ride scoping out what they wanted to do next. By the time they landed, they knew they were making a beeline for the row of food booths set up along one side of the dome. With so many options, it was difficult to decide what they wanted to try. Mia studied the booths suspiciously.

"What's wrong?" Carson asked, reaching out to accept a giant soft pretzel from one of the attendants.

"Is it even real?" Mia asked. "I mean, you saw them. Elmhurst and the other teachers just kind of poofed all this stuff into being."

"Poofed? Is that the technical term?" Vivi asked. "I've gone all these years calling it magic."

"Be quiet, Vivi," Luna said. "Eat your candy apple."

Even if Vivi had wanted to respond, the lure of the apple she had chosen was too much, and she sank her teeth into it happily.

"The food is real," Zander assured Mia. "It was brought in from somewhere, not just…poofed into existence."

"That's a relief. I think," Mia said.

"And you sound like an idiot saying poofed by the way." Carson hooted with laughter.

"There you are." Cassia came up to them with a large cardboard container of nachos in one hand. "I've been looking for you. Have you tried the nachos? They're amazing." Cassia picked up one of the nachos, loaded it with the gooey cheese sauce, and stuffed it in her mouth.

Mia chuckled and reached for one. She took a bite and groaned. "Ohhhh, that *is* good," she said. She reached for another. "Have you been enjoying the party?"

"I have. I'm technically supposed to be guarding, but I think that includes going down the giant inflatable slide and eating as much as I can get my hands on," Cassia told her.

"I agree," Mia said.

Cassia slid her eyes over to Vivi. "And from that giant inflatable slide, I saw something interesting."

Vivi glanced at her innocently. "What?"

"Let's just agree to keep hands, feet, torso, and head, inside all rides from now on."

Vivi nodded and turned away, going back to eating her apple as the others laughed.

"What are you doing next?" Mia asked.

"I have to keep wandering around, making sure everything is fine Enjoy the rest of the celebration. I'll catch up with you tomorrow."

They hugged, and Mia snagged one more chip before her guardian walked away. Mia headed for the booth for her own container of nachos, intending to share them with the others, so she still had room for as many of the other treats as she could fit in her stomach.

CHAPTER TWENTY-FOUR

"So, I have to ask you," Zander said, a while later, as they waited for their turns on the giant inflatable slide.

"What's that?" Mia asked.

The line in front of them moved up, and she followed. She and Zander were the only two of the five who had decided to do the slide. The others had headed for the hall of mirrors, instead. Which had never been Mia's favorite activity at a carnival. It was disorienting, and she hated that feeling.

Of course, she probably wouldn't feel as much that way now as she used to. Ever since finding Cassia, her entire life had become about being somewhat disoriented and having to try to find her way. Maybe now it would be more amusing to her.

"Was it you?" Zander said.

She threw him a strange look over her shoulder. "Is this some sort of live-action game of *Clue* I wasn't told about?"

"No."

"Good." Mia followed the progress of the line again. "Because if it was, you would be a terrible player."

Zander laughed. "Well, thanks for that. No, I mean, did you have any hand in us winning the slamball championship?"

"What do you mean?"

"You know what I'm talking about. Elmhurst really needed the morale boost of winning. Then they managed to pull it off in a game like that. Did you have something to do with that?"

"No. Are you kidding?" Mia shook her head.

Zander leaned closer. "You can tell me. I wouldn't tell anybody."

Mia made an exasperated sound and turned to glare at him as the line stopped moving. "I didn't do anything, Zander. I didn't use my skills at the game, period. I never have, and never would."

"That's not really true."

"What do you mean?"

"I know you used your skills at the game in Las Vegas. The one we watched against the vampires," Zander said.

Mia was confused. She remembered the game, but she couldn't figure out what he meant. "What are you talking about? I barely even knew what slamball was when we were watching that game. How would I use any powers to affect it?"

"What I'm wondering is how you were able to penetrate the enchantments put around the court to prevent people from doing things like that," he said.

"Things like what?" Mia asked, exasperated. Zander appeared convinced, but the whole situation was a blank to her. "All I did was watch the game. I didn't use any of my skills to do anything."

"You seriously didn't mean to manipulate the game against the vampires in Las Vegas?" he asked.

She shook her head. "No, I didn't."

"And you didn't have anything to do with us winning the Championship?" he continued.

This shake of her head was more adamant. "No. I have no idea how a game would even be influenced. I didn't do anything. At least, I don't think I did. You're freaking me out a little. I would certainly hope I would know if I did something like that."

His eyes narrowed, and he stared at her. It didn't seem like he was searching her to see if she was telling the truth. It was more like he was going back through his own memories of the game they watched in Las Vegas, and then the competition that unfolded here at Elmhurst. His mind flipped through all the games and those moments he believed she had manipulated.

Finally, he gave a slight, resigned shrug. "The game was incredible, but it was neck-and-neck the entire time. It's not like any completely miraculous points were scored, though. I guess if you were really going to affect the game, you wouldn't let it go that far and make it so close. Especially with Carson right on the edge like he was through that whole final."

"Do you really think he had a betting pool going?" Mia asked.

"Where did you hear that?"

"I overheard some of the girls in the bathroom talking about it earlier." Mia's nose scrunched, and in her mind, she went over what she had overheard. She was confident the girls had been talking about their Carson.

Zander shook his head, and they climbed a little farther up the tower supporting the slide. They were almost at the top now, and Mia looked around the carnival in search of the others. She didn't see them near the hall of mirrors, so she assumed they were still inside.

"No, I don't think so. Carson wouldn't do something like that. He's too straight-laced to get into wagers. Getting caught doing something like that wouldn't look good on his applications when he's trying to get into college or work for the Embassy in New York. Besides, I'm fairly certain Vivi started spreading that rumor just so people would show up at our dorm in the middle of the night to irritate us," he told her.

"That sounds like Vivi."

It was Mia's turn to descend the slide, and Zander watched her take her place in front of the opening. She appeared nervous, and he laughed.

"Go on, Mia," he said. "You have battled far more difficult adversaries than a giant puffy slide."

She smiled and dropped onto the green-and-orange striped surface. His mind ran over their conversation as he listened to her squeal with delight on her way down. He had been almost positive she had done something to help the school win the final game. Not that she would have interfered enough to have gotten in the way of the game actually being played.

She could have changed things up a little to give their home team a leg up against the visitors, but Mia was steadfast in her denial, and he wanted to believe her. She did seem clueless about her influence over the game in Las Vegas and determined to deny she had anything to do with these games, either.

Of course, her denial didn't necessarily mean she didn't do it. Just because she hadn't purposely created an enchantment, or used a spell, didn't mean she hadn't had some influence over the outcome of the game.

As she hit the bottom of the slide and he positioned himself, Zander made a mental note to test the impressive halfling's power of persuasion. On several occasions, she had appeared to be achieving things, or causing things to happen, without willfully doing it, but merely because she had wanted it to happen. Desire could be a very strong power, and he wanted to know how much she could do simply by the force of desiring it to happen.

Desiring something to happen and making it come to be through that desire was a full-fae gift. Halflings had to say certain words or perform specific enchantments in order for anything to happen. Halflings couldn't simply wish these things to be. They weren't genies or djinn. He wanted to know how much control she had over this ability, and how much she might be able to do even when she didn't have that control.

"Go ahead." The attendant perched at the top of the slide waved him through.

Zander grabbed onto the pole at the entrance to the slide and used it to propel himself at a faster speed than Mia had. Mia was waiting for him at the bottom when he landed on the cushion at the end of the slide.

'I think the others may have gotten lost in there. Let's go find them," Mia said.

He agreed, and they walked across the carnival. A few seconds later, Dan and Steve swooped over to them.

"This is fantastic," Steve said. "They should leave this up all the time."

"I don't think anything would ever get done around here if they left this up all the time," Mia said with a laugh. She studied the statues more closely and realized Dan's face was sticky. "Did you eat cotton candy?"

He nodded. "I've never had it before. It's not like we need to eat, but I'm enjoying trying things."

At Thanksgiving dinner, she had watched them delight in the new textures and flavors of the food, not even registering that they had never eaten those things before. Or anything, for all she knew. It was odd to think about them existing for so long, yet having such limited experience. Being freed from their pedestals had suddenly introduced them to a whole new reality and a world of possibilities. It wasn't just about being able to fly, or seeing more of the academy than they ever had. They were learning new things about themselves and finding out what it was like to really live.

In so many ways, Mia felt like she could understand that. To her, coming to the academy. Just that quickly, an entirely new side of her life had opened up, and she had discovered what it was like to really live as her true self.

That sentiment took on somewhat of a dark turn a few minutes later when she, Zander, and the gargoyles entered the hall of mirrors in search of the other three. Mia could have waited outside, but she was determined to experiment and see if the changes in her life had also changed the way she saw the house of mirrors.

Now she was realizing that was far too optimistic a hope. She was just as freaked out and uncomfortable walking through the narrow corridors of mirrors as she ever had been. Maybe even more.

It was reassuring to have Zander close behind her, but soon he took a turn, and she lost his many reflections. She whipped around, but she couldn't see anyone. It was only her and the dozens of reflections of her face appearing around her. Every direction she looked, there were more of her.

Mia's breath grew shallow and fast, and she struggled to calm it down. Her head was growing woozy, and she moved more quickly in hopes of finding anyone. She didn't want to yell out for them. The familiar sensation of being watched scraped along her skin, but if she shouted, she would only be giving herself up.

She ran along the hallways and took every turn she could find. Finally, she burst into an octagonal room that reminded her of the portal room inside the academy. Dan and Steve stood in front of one of the mirrored panels, making faces at each other. They hadn't quite gotten control of their stone features enough to dramatically change their expressions, but even the slight shifts and their tongues sticking out were funny.

"There she is," Zander said a second later when the other four streamed out of a hallway toward her.

"Are you okay, Mia?" Luna asked.

Mia tried to shake off the discomfort. "I thought I might like these places now, but I definitely don't. They're still just as weird."

"What don't you like about them?" Carson asked. "It's just mirrors. You look in a mirror every day."

"Yes, *a* mirror. Just one at a time. Not a hundred. It's just creepy. I feel like I'm staring at myself. No matter what I do, I'm right there, staring back. It's like I'm being forced to confront myself and everything I've ever done. I can't get away from it. I have to look at it and think about who I am and who I'm supposed to be, what I've done or should have done. Or maybe shouldn't have done. What I'll eventually have to do. It's all right here, and it won't leave me alone." A shiver slithered down Mia's spine.

"Poetic," Vivi said.

Mia hadn't meant to pour all that out, but the words wouldn't stop. She wrapped her arms around herself. "Maybe that's why I've never been good at poetry," she quipped, trying to dispel some of the tension. "Maybe poets just have to be in really uncomfortable situations *all* the time."

"I think that's pretty much the consensus for most of them." Zander grinned at her and reached for her hand. "Come on. We'll get you out of here."

He guided her through the corridors with Luna close behind, as though they were creating a protective barrier. They had already gone through most of the maze looking for her and had discovered the way out, so it was easy to get to the exit.

Mia instantly felt better when they left the small structure and returned to the real world. She drew a deep breath and stared up at the top of the dome. The teachers hadn't put the colored panels back after opening the party. Instead, they had created something from a dream.

The reimagined sky was full of bright stars and pillows of snowy white clouds. Snow was still falling, but when it came close to the dome, it was blown away, never reaching the holes in the dome that vented the smoke from the fire pit and the cooking booths.

"I need to learn how to do something like that," she said.

"Like what?" Vivi asked.

Mia pointed up. "Look at the snow. It's not getting in or gathering on the top of the dome at all. I want to be able to do that. You know, for future needs." She chuckled as the others nodded.

"Can you imagine what we could make if we keep getting stronger?" Carson asked. "With the Power of Five, we could make a dome like this on an even bigger scale. We could make it large enough to cover the entire campus. Or even the whole town."

Luna giggled. "Perfect. Just what we would need. A town in a bubble."

"It could have its uses," Mia said. "But I don't think we're ready for that, yet."

"Not yet," Zander said. "But I know what I'm ready for."

"What?" Vivi asked.

"More food," the guys said in unison and headed back toward the booths.

The girls groaned and laughed. They felt like they had eaten their weight in carnival food already, but the guys were bottomless pits. They followed the boys to the food and sampled a few bites of each thing they received before making their way over to a cluster of games.

Dan and Steve were determined to try their luck at a couple of the games of chance. The first few times, they didn't get anywhere, and Mia could see they were becoming frustrated. She remembered what Zander had said about her being able to use her skills to manipulate the slamball game and ensure the winner. What if she might be able to do the same to nudge the outcome of one of these games a little so the gargoyles could have the fun of winning?

Before she could do anything, the ball Steve had thrown went right into the basket he was aiming for. He released a thrilled *whoop* a moment before Dan's water gun propelled a little duck right to the top of a tower to hit a bell. She smiled. She wasn't going to have to try to intervene after all. She was walking up to congratulate them when, from the corner of her eye, she caught Zander staring at her. She didn't turn to look back at him.

The next day, after all the non-Elmhurst students were gone, Cassia called Mia and her friends into Elmhurst's office. "I was able to find the video from the Louvre. Someone had erased it, but they didn't think to erase the off-site back-ups." She chuckled. "I expected better of him."

"Of who?" Mia's brow furrowed and stared at Cassia expectantly.

"Narco. He's the fae who's been trailing you."

Mia nodded and wrapped her arms around her torso. She had known it was Narco, but she had hoped she was wrong.

"Who is he?" Zander, acting as the leader of their group, stood with a worried expression on his face.

Cassia glanced at the headmistress, who nodded. "He's one of the best bounty hunters the Unseelie Court has." She looked at Vivi and Carson, whose expressions were blank. "You two haven't heard of him?"

Vivi thought it over for a moment. "Yeah, I guess I have, but why would he be following us? Or be after Mia? It doesn't make any sense."

"Yeah, if he's this big-shot bounty hunter, why is he interested in halfling students?" Carson scratched his head.

The bounty hunter in the room crossed her arms over her chest and glared out the window. "That's exactly what I want to find out."

CHAPTER TWENTY-FIVE

E veryone was still talking about the party two weeks later when the semester ended. The visiting schools had left the day after the carnival to return to their own campuses for the end of the semester, and the academy felt too quiet.

Even though the other students had only been on campus with them for the duration of the championships, the halflings had grown used to having so many more people around, and the fun of making new friends. It was a letdown to have them all gone and be made to wait even longer for Christmas break. Every day, classes dragged on, and the teachers seemed to pile more work on the students as if wanting to fill up every possible second they had available.

As soon as the semester ended, they would be on their way and would have two blissful weeks without school.

A few students had grumbled that the teachers seemed to be making up for creating the championship party. As if they didn't want it to look like they were going soft and could be persuaded into fun and frolic from now on.

Not that Mia ever made the mistake of thinking that was a

possibility. She and the other five were very familiar with how intense the teachers could be. This was especially true when the teachers had a lot to accomplish in a short time, or when they believed the students weren't applying themselves enough.

But finally, the days had gone by, and the wait was over. It was the last day of the semester, and everyone was going off in different directions for their break. Carson and Zander had already left. Their parents had picked them up early so they could head out of town to spend the holiday with their human families.

Zander had laughed as he told her many of his cousins didn't know he was half-fae. Sometimes he would mess with them, using little enchantments or small spells to play pranks. When she said she didn't think he was the type to play pranks and asked if it was allowed for them to use magic when they were among the humans, Zander had just winked at her and walked away.

That wink had made Mia's cheeks burn, and her fingertips tingle, but she didn't allow herself to think about it too much. Luna was waiting with Mia until Cassia was ready to leave. Many of the other guards were already gone, having left campus when the visiting schools had departed.

Cassia and a few others had decided to stay and provide continued security until the semester ended. That day she was just finishing up, making her rounds, checking over the campus with Elmhurst to ensure the school was secure and ready to be mostly closed down for the holidays. There would still be a few people around, but not enough to keep watch over the entire campus.

"I bet my mother has already started making gingerbread," Luna said wistfully. "She bakes up about a million gingerbread men. And women, and children, and animals, and occasionally even Halloween shapes and turkeys, if she's made too much dough and is tired of using the same cookie cutters. We have so much fun decorating them."

"That sounds like fun," Mia replied. "I've never made ginger-bread before."

"What? I'll be sure to save you some when you come to my house after Christmas," she said. "We'll have a great time."

Mia smiled at her as Vivi came into the common area lugging several bags.

"Are you moving out?" Luna asked with a laugh.

"Not that lucky. No, I'm just never sure what's actually going to happen when I go home for a break. So I would rather be prepared with everything I might need than to go into it blind," Vivi said.

"You're still going skiing with your father, right?" Mia asked.

"That's the plan. I talked to him yesterday, and he was still saying he'll be here this afternoon to pick me up and head for the slopes."

She wasn't letting it show, and definitely wouldn't say anything about it, but Vivi was excited to finally be going on her skiing trip with her father. As he had said he would, he had continued to check in on Vivi, her progress, and her behavior.

Principal Elmhurst hadn't hesitated to tell him how impressed she was with Vivi's progress and her cooperation with the others in the group. The headmistress knew how the fae man felt about his daughter associating with Seelie halflings, but she had emphasized how well they were working together and the advancements Vivi was making.

She had agreed not to give any details about the group's excursion to the museum or creating the portal. Her offer to give them the freedom to experiment and push the limitations of their abilities still stood, which meant hiding some of the realities of their activities from people on the outside. Even parents.

Vivi's father was so pleased by what he had heard that he'd reinstated their skiing trip and had even sent Vivi money to buy a new wardrobe to bring with her. It appeared she had taken full advantage of that perk.

Mia laughed when almost immediately, one of the staff came into the room to inform Vivi that her father had arrived. Vivi groaned and stood, grabbing her luggage again to haul it away.

"Merry Christmas, Vivi," Luna and Mia said in unison.

Vivi rolled her eyes and glanced at them with a slight smile. "Merry Christmas, guys. I'll see you in a couple weeks."

"Have fun skiing," Mia said.

Luna didn't have any reason to rush away from campus since she was staying at home in town with her mother. With a hug and a promise to meet the day after Christmas, they parted ways.

It felt strange to be away from the other four for an entire week. Mia loved spending time with Cassia, and though she missed her father, she and her guardian began to create new Christmas traditions together.

One of her favorites was staying up late into the night drinking peppermint hot chocolate and watching movies in the matching gaudy holiday-pajamas Cassia had picked out for them. But despite all the fun, Mia was excited to stay with Luna for the week after Christmas and was even looking forward to returning to campus.

Vivi arrived two days before classes started again, and Luna and Mia went to meet up with her. They were outside the library, visiting with Dan and Steve the next day when Carson and Zander ran toward them.

Finally back together, the group of five exchanged hugs and high fives, laughing and grinning as they talked about their breaks. Their voices overlapped, and they grew louder and louder as if they had saved up everything they would have said to each other during the break and were letting it all out.

"I know it's only been two weeks, but I feel so out of practice," Carson admitted.

"You didn't use any magic over Christmas?" Luna asked.

He shook his head. "My mom and step-dad were watching me

pretty closely. They know I'm getting more powerful and are worried I'll do something as a prank that could end up hurting someone or causing trouble."

"I did a few enchantments and spells, but it's good to be back together. It feels like so long since we've tried to combine our magic to do anything big," Luna agreed.

"Want to try something?" Mia asked. "Just to get back in the groove?"

"Do you think it's safe?" Zander asked. "With the guards gone, Elmhurst might have more rules and restrictions she may want to have us follow this semester."

"So, let's go talk to her and find out," Vivi suggested.

They said goodbye to the gargoyles, promising to see them later, and went to the headmistress's office. She greeted the happy   excited-to-be-back-and-ready-for-the-next-semester group of students.

"We were wondering..." Mia spoke slowly. "If we could start practicing together again. As strange as it sounds, we realized we missed each other, and we want to start working on the Power of Five again."

"But we didn't know if that was safe or if anything may have happened while we were gone," Luna said.

The headmistress shook her head. "Thank you for asking. That shows a level of maturity you wouldn't have exhibited earlier in the school year. There has been no sign of Narco or any of his associates. The campus is secure. For now, you can consider it safe and return to your normal practice. But be cautious. Be aware of your surroundings, and don't hesitate to tell me if you see anything strange. Other than that, get back to work."

The five halflings smiled at each other and hurried outside to practice. As they rushed to the fields behind the academy building, Hazel stepped out from around the corner. No one but Dan and Steve had paid her much attention, but she had been back on campus for almost a week.

As soon as the academy had allowed students back into the dorms, she had returned and settled in, not knowing when Mia would return. She wanted to be ready and not miss anything.

CHAPTER TWENTY-SIX

Hazel was still watching Mia, though she didn't want to. Spying on her made Hazel feel guilty. Mia had never done anything to her, and she had actually gone out of her way to help Hazel. She'd been there for Hazel when Sariah had tormented her and had even welcomed her to sit with the group of five during the slamball championship.

Hazel felt terrible about betraying Mia's trust the way she was. She wanted to find some way to tell the other girl what was going on, but she couldn't. José wouldn't permit it. The control the vampire had over her wouldn't allow her to reveal what was going on, so she could do nothing to let Mia know.

It was becoming harder and harder on her the longer the spying dragged out. She talked to Marcus about it, telling him how the situation was making her feel and what she was going through, but it didn't make any difference. Marcus seemed fine with it.

In fact, he was more than fine with it. He was very happy with his situation. His loyalty to his vampire master was going to ensure that Marcus got everything he ever wanted. As long as he did what José told him to, he would be accepted into the best college. The day after graduation, he would be hired for a cushy job that he could hang onto throughout his adulthood and just keep advancing. It was everything most of the halflings could ever ask for, and it was being handed right to him.

Of course, this wasn't merely a magnanimous response from the vampire to his servant. He would want Marcus placed in a high position as a reward to him for his loyalty and his work, but that wasn't the only benefit. A job like that would also give him the ideal opportunity to continue spying for as long as José wanted him to.

Hazel didn't want it. She didn't want any of it. She set herself to find out how the vampire was controlling her, and how she could release herself from that control.

She had been going to the library every night for a couple of weeks when the gargoyles began to take notice. Steve and Dan descended from their pedestals and glided around the sides of the building, peering into the windows until they were able to see what she was doing. Hazel sat by herself at the table farthest back, only one small green lamp glowing in the corner, illuminating her book. Despite bad lighting and their distance, Dan was able to see what she was reading.

"Why would this halfling be reading about vampire thralls?" he asked. "Not just about vampire thralls, but about how to get over them?"

"It's probably something for one of her classes," Steve suggested. "She's writing a paper or doing a project."

Dan shook his head. "She wouldn't have to come here so many times for something like that. And even if she did, why doesn't she have anything with her? She's not taking any notes or writing anything. She's just reading. There's something going on. I think she might be what Cinder warned us about."

Steve moved away from the window, and Dan glanced up at him. "What are you doing?" Dan asked.

"I'm going to fly around some more," Steve replied. "Are you coming?"

"No," Dan said. "I'm going to stick around here. I want to keep an eye on Hazel and find out what she's up to."

"All right, I'll check and see if there's anything out here that might explain what's going on," Steve said.

He flew off, and Dan returned to watching Hazel. A few minutes later, she pulled her phone from her pocket and checked it. Seemingly startled by the time, she stuffed it back into her pocket, scooped her book off the table, and hurried through the library.

Dan glided along the side of the building again, monitoring her movements through the windows to see where she was going. He briefly thought she might be leaving, but instead, she went to the front of the library and into a dark corner. No one else was in the library at this hour; Elmhurst left it open for later hours during the second half of the school year, but few students actually took advantage of it until closer to mid-terms.

But Hazel seemed to be there for a purpose. She sat on a high-backed chair and stared around nervously for a few seconds, as though waiting for someone. Finally, Marcus joined her. He said something to her, and she nodded before standing and following him outside.

Dan followed them discretely into the shadows of a nearby building, where they stood close to each other to talk. Both kept looking back toward the library as if they thought someone else might be inside.

"What is so important that you needed to talk to me tonight?" Marcus demanded.

"We need to talk about what's going on with José," Hazel replied in a conspiratorial whisper.

Marcus rolled his eyes. "Not this again, Hazel."

"Hear me out, Marcus. Listen to me. José has us under his control.

We are under the effect of a vampire thrall, and that is what's making us do all these things for him. I read all about it. But we can get out of it. It doesn't have to be this way," she insisted. "We just need help."

"I don't want out. Why don't you understand that?" Marcus snapped. "This is good for me. Working for José is going to open up the world for me. I want that. I don't want help getting away from him. I want the promises of a bright future. I want to know when I get out of this place, I'll be able to get into college and have a job waiting for me. I want the assurance of a good life. Those are all things José is offering me that would have been totally out of reach for me earlier this year."

"It doesn't have to be through him, Marcus. I know you want a good future, but this isn't the only way."

"What would *you* know about it?" Marcus demanded. "It's not as if what he could offer really matters to you that much. Those things were never out of your reach to begin with."

Hazel knew it was true. She'd always had the promise of a bright future. Her father would see to that. "It might be different for me, but that still doesn't mean we have to keep going like this. What if what he's asking of us keeps getting worse? What are his limits? What are yours? The longer we stay under his thrall, the stronger and more intense it will get. I don't want to end up in an even more frightening situation than we're already in. Besides, don't you have any feelings about Mia?"

"What do you mean, feelings about Mia?" Marcus asked. "What kind of feelings should I have about her?"

"She hasn't done anything wrong. Not to either of us. In fact, she's been really nice. She's protected me and tried to be my friend. There's been nothing to show that she deserves this," Hazel said.

"It's not for us to decide what she deserves. This is up to José, and this is what he wants."

"But that's just it. Why? Why does he want it? He's never given us any sort of reason why he would want to put her through this.

He's never even told us the full reason why he wants us to spy on her and report everything back to him, to begin with."

"He has no reason to. It's not any of our business. It doesn't matter why he wants the information about her. All that matters is that he does, and he's having us get it for him," Marcus argued.

Hazel shook her head. "I just can't do this anymore. I don't want to keep sneaking around, spying on her."

"You're not going to mess this up for me," he growled. He started walking away from her.

"Where are you going?"

He didn't respond, and Dan immediately flew off to find Steve. After telling him what the two halflings had discussed, he sent Steve to follow Marcus while he went to talk to Mia. She needed to know what was going on.

Steve stayed high in the sky as he searched for Marcus, wanting to find him as quickly as possible without the halfling spotting him. By the time he caught up to him at the far edge of one of the campus fields, Marcus was already with José.

They stood close together as Marcus spoke quickly, his hands animated. "She is determined to stop helping you."

José didn't look concerned. "Don't worry. There's nothing she can do. No matter how much Hazel wants to, she can't break my enchantment. She is forever my slave. But if she is trying to resist, she may prove to be an obstacle. Keep an eye on her and make sure she doesn't get in the way."

With that, the vampire stalked away, leaving Marcus to walk back to the academy building alone.

CHAPTER TWENTY-SEVEN

Mia paced across her dorm room. Her hands tingled, and her head buzzed with anger. She couldn't believe what Dan told her the night before. She had decided not to approach the others so late, thinking if she had a night of sleep first, it would give her a chance to calm down and think through the situation rationally.

That's not what happened. Instead, she woke up angrier. Everything the gargoyle had told her sank in, and her fury split in two. She was livid for herself and with the threat against her. But now she was even angrier for Hazel.

Mia could take care of herself if she had to. She had already proved herself many times and was only becoming stronger, the more she practiced her skills. Hazel was different. The young halfling didn't have the same power Mia had, nor the amount of strength and support.

"He can't do this to her," she growled. "He can't keep her as his slave just because she isn't strong enough to fight him off. That's why he targeted her. He knew he could get control of her and use her against me."

"It isn't necessarily about strength. Marcus is a more powerful halfling than Hazel is in many ways, and Dan and Steve said he's in on it, too," Luna pointed out.

"But he's not bothered by it. He's happy to do the vampire's bidding if it means giving him a leg up on a better future. He'll gleefully toss me under a moving train if it's going to secure him a place at his college of choice and a good job. He doesn't want to escape José's control, so it doesn't matter. But Hazel does. She doesn't want him pushing her around anymore," Mia said. "So she shouldn't have to go through it."

"So, what are we going to do?" Luna asked. "How do we stop it?"

"If she's in a true thrall, it's not going to be easy," Vivi said. "Vampires aren't exactly known for their gentle persuasion. When Hazel says she is a slave to this guy, that's what she means."

"But there has to be some way to break the thrall. There has to be something we can do to get her away from him," Mia insisted.

"We'll find a way," Zander assured her.

"Why don't we go talk to her?" Mia suggested. "She might be able to tell us something that could help."

The five hurried from the dorm room and moved around campus searching for Hazel. They finally found her hunched in the library, reading the book the gargoyles had told them about.

"Hazel," Mia said.

Hazel glanced up and gave a slight gasp. "Mia," she said, trying to push the book out of sight. "What are you doing here?"

"You don't have to hide the book, Hazel. We know what's going on. That's why we came to talk to you."

Color splashed across the younger girl's cheeks, and she opened her mouth, about to say something, but no sound came out.

"Come on," Luna told her. "We don't know who might be listening. Let's go back to our room."

Hazel was still dumbstruck as she followed the five to the

dorms. There, on the edge of Mia's bed, Hazel sat staring at them. "What is it you know about?" she asked hesitantly. There was almost a pleading sound to her voice, as though she desperately wanted to say something else, but needed those words to convey it for her.

"Dan and Steve overheard you talking to Marcus. So we know about José," Mia said. "We want to help you."

Hazel opened her mouth, and her eyes widened. She closed it and opened it again, but her eyes only grew wider. They were almost frantic.

"What?" Luna asked. "What's wrong?"

Hazel strained, her eyes filling with tears. She clawed at her throat.

"Is she all right? Is she choking?" Carson asked.

Hazel shook her head.

"No. That's not what's wrong. Ask her something else. Talk about something else," Mia said.

"What did you have for breakfast, Hazel?" Zander asked.

"French toast."

They all stared at the girl, and she exhaled slowly.

"She can't talk about José," Mia said. "She can't say anything about him."

"Write it down," Luna suggested. "Write down everything about him and how you got here."

They handed her a piece of paper and a pen, but her hand wouldn't move. Hazel stared at it, trying to force it to form words, but it shook and ached, not doing what she wanted it to.

"I can't," she said.

"We have to do something," Mia insisted. "This man is her jailer, and she can't even tell us what's going on so we can help her." She rested her hand on Hazel's shoulder. "I'm going to figure this out, Hazel. I'm going to find a way to break the spell binding you to this guy. You will be free."

The words were no sooner out of her mouth than a loud

popping sounded, and Hazel cried out. Falling from the end of the bed, she landed on the floor and began to writhe, her body contorting and bending as she whimpered in pain. The agony was so extreme she couldn't even scream. She could only gag and fight to breathe.

Instantly terrified, Mia dropped to her knees and put her hands on Hazel. "Hazel! What's going on? What can I do?" she cried.

"I'm going to get Elmhurst," Luna said. She rushed from the room and along the hall. A communication sphere embedded in the wall would immediately connect to the headmistress and ensure she reached them as quickly as possible.

The room filled with the sound of Hazel's pain as the four halflings tried to figure out what was happening and what they could do. Their voices overlapped and blended, making it difficult to decipher any specific words.

Finally, Vivi held out her hands to stop them all. "This is because of the vampire," she said. "Mia removed the spell, but because José didn't do it, there was a price to pay. This is Hazel's price."

"So, we're just supposed to accept it?" Mia demanded. "We're supposed to just stand here and let her suffer until it's done because she deserves it for wanting to be free?"

"That's not what she said," Carson said, trying to calm Mia.

"It's not what I meant," Vivi said. "I— I'm worried about her, too."

It was a surprising revelation for all of them, but the way her eyebrows were knit together, and how much darker her eyes had grown had revealed how concerned she actually was.

"You are?" Zander asked.

"Yeah," Vivi spat. "I don't get it, either. Hazel was never a friend of mine. She's more of a nuisance, really. But now I'm worried about her. I don't understand why I would feel so bad for the girl, but there it is. Maybe it's part of the spell."

Mia shook her head. Vivi would never change. She couldn't even deal with a few minutes of normal compassionate emotion for another living being without being convinced something was wrong.

"Mia, try to make it go away," Zander said. "Like we talked about. Like slamball."

She didn't understand at first, but it sank in. Focusing on Hazel, she put all her energy and concentration into wishing for the pain to go away. She wanted it with everything in her and sent that thought out toward the girl. A few minutes into this, Elmhurst ran down the hallway and into the room.

"What's happening?" she asked. They explained it to her, and Mia looked up, eyes filled with pain. "I'm trying to make it stop," she said. "But it's not doing any good."

Hazel wasn't reacting as strongly, though, so some of the pain might have dissipated. But she was still writhing, still groaning. Elmhurst immediately dropped onto the floor and put her hand over Hazel's heart. She closed her eyes and whispered something Mia couldn't understand.

"Ancient tongue," Zander whispered to her. "Very few fae still know it."

When she finished, the headmistress glanced at Mia and nodded. Seconds later, Hazel's face relaxed and smoothed out. Her breathing calmed, and it was obvious she wasn't in pain anymore.

Relief washed over Mia, but seconds later it melted under a wave of grief and guilt. "I'm sorry," she whispered. "I'm so sorry."

"Why are you sorry?" Hazel asked. "You didn't do anything. This isn't your fault."

"But I couldn't stop it. I tried so hard. I did everything I could. Really, I did," Mia told her.

"Mia, what are you talking about?" Elmhurst asked.

"Like with the gargoyles and the snow falling on Narco. I

wanted the pain to go away. I wanted Hazel to be all right, and I couldn't make it happen."

"That isn't your fault," the headmistress told her, taking hold of her shoulders and looking directly into her eyes. "You didn't do this, and it wasn't your responsibility to make the pain stop. You already did something incredible by breaking that spell. You can't expect yourself to do something some full fae struggle to master."

"If it wasn't for me…"

"No, Mia," Hazel said. "Don't think that way. This is José. Not you."

"Tell us everything," Elmhurst said. "We'll figure out what to do from there."

Hazel told them the entire story, explaining how she fell under the enslavement of the vampire José and what he wanted her and Marcus to do. The headmistress confirmed that Marcus was already gone, having disappeared off-campus, probably right after talking with José. Elmhurst left with a warning that it was time to work harder, to push themselves further and build their skills, especially Mia. Something was coming, and they needed to be prepared.

For the next few weeks, Mia dove headlong into familiarizing herself with her powers, polishing her skills, and learning more about the world she belonged to. She worked as hard as she could, sometimes pushing herself into exhaustion so complete she could barely move. But it didn't discourage her. She wouldn't allow the difficulty of it to hold her back. This was what she was meant for, and she was going to do it.

She wasn't in it alone. It wasn't only the other four of the group of five or even Professor Elmhurst. Dan and Steve had dedicated themselves to being a part of the cause in every way they could. That meant the instant he was allowed off his pedestal at night, Dan came to Mia and stayed with her, and also sat outside her window while she slept. Steve spent every night flying over the campus and the nearby town, making sure there were no sightings of Narco or vampires nearby.

Everything was quiet. But that was the problem. It was far too quiet. Something was coming, and they all worried about what it might be.

CHAPTER TWENTY-EIGHT

It seemed as though it would take forever, but finally, spring came to Montana. Mia was beginning to think the snow would never go away, and she would always be stuck in a perpetual winter.

"I've seen that movie," Luna joked when Mia shared the thought. "It was cute."

"Maybe if you get to wear a fabulous dress and have magical powers that can control everything," Mia snapped.

Carson shot her a bemused look, and Mia realized what she had said.

"Yeah," Carson said. "It would be so strange and completely out of my frame of reference for you to have magical powers that can control things."

Mia kicked some of the sloshy, partially-melted snow from the sidewalk at him. He curved away, and it hit his shoulder with a wet plop. He gasped at the cold, and she snickered, but her laughter stopped when he leaned down to scoop up a handful of the slush. He turned to Mia, and she squealed.

She took off running away from him, heading for the field behind the academy building. It was still clean after being abandoned since before Christmas break. Now that the warmer spring sun was finally starting to melt the snow away, it was the perfect spot for a snowball battle to celebrate the last reminders of winter.

Mia managed to duck out of the way of the loose snowball that came flying at her but gasped when it stopped in midair and changed direction to come racing back toward her. It splattered in the middle of her chest, some of the bits of ice slipping down into her coat and making her shiver.

"No fair using magic snowballs!" she shouted.

"Why not?" Carson asked. "That was never a rule."

"Yeah, Mia." Vivi bent to grab her own handful of snow. "You're at Elmhurst Academy now. Everything has magic, even the snowball fights. It just makes everything so much better."

Mia held up a finger at the Unseelie girl. "Vivi," she said in warning, "we're supposed to be in this together."

Vivi grinned at her, lifting her hand to launch the snowball. At the last second, she turned and threw it at the back of Zander's head. The Seelie halfling shouted and whipped around, grabbing up more snow as he went. He threw the handful, and it broke into several small snowballs that showered down on the girls. Carson laughed loudly, and the fight was on. Vivi enchanted some of the snow to form itself into a fort, but it was melting so fast it couldn't stay solid, so she had to keep rebuilding.

Mia stared around her frantically. Luna stood several yards away in the middle of the field. "Luna!" she shouted. "What are you doing? We're getting pummeled over here."

"I'm making snowmen!" she yelled in reply.

"Snowmen?" Vivi demanded. "Why are you doing that?"

"Because they are fun." Mia smiled when Luna moved out of the way to present her snowman.

The two boys stopped their full-on snowball assault and turned to the snowman. As soon as they looked at it, the snowman melted into the ground. The snow spread out into a wide puddle, and from the pool of water, three snowmen emerged.

"That's a cute trick," Carson said.

"It's not done," Luna said.

On cue, the three snowmen melted, and the puddle grew wider. From it, six more snowmen appeared. Only this time, they were bigger, and each was holding an armful of snowballs. They each grabbed one and threw them in unison at the guys. All three girls released delighted screams as the guys thrashed about trying to dive out of the way of the sudden hail of snowballs.

"I want to play!"

Mia glanced up at the sound of the voice. Cinder was fluttering toward them. Instead of making her own snowball, she sent a blast of magic at some of the ones the guys were trying to form and send back toward the girls. They melted when she looked at them, creating little patches of grass where the remainder of the snow disappeared under the heated water.

The snowmen Luna made ran out of snowballs, and Mia enchanted them to start moving across the field toward the guys. Behind them, another row sprung up, then another, and another. Soon the ground was half-filled with melting soldiers advancing on Zander and Carson.

As they threw enchanted snowballs at them, they burst into flame from the magic of the little pixie giggling and flying around above them. They mostly evaporated before reaching the guys, but it was still fun for Mia to watch them scrambling and trying to fight back.

Mia held onto the memory of that fun early spring afternoon a few weeks later when all the snow was gone and the warmer season had officially set in. Their coats, gloves, hats, scarves, and boots finally put away for the year, the five halflings spent more time outside enjoying the sunlight on their skin.

As the days grew longer, a strange feeling settled over the campus. It wasn't the lack of clothing layers making Mia feel exposed. Everywhere she went, she felt eyes on her. She was being watched, her every move monitored, and it had her on edge.

She let it go on for almost two weeks before she finally went to Elmhurst. The headmistress ushered the group of five halflings into her office and closed the door. Checking to make sure no one else was around to listen in, she sat at her desk and invited Mia to tell her what was happening. Mia explained the feeling and how many students she had noticed watching her.

"I think now that he's lost Hazel, José got himself new spies," she told the headmistress.

"That seems like a safe assumption," Elmhurst confirmed. "Do you have any guesses as to who it might be?"

Mia hesitated before she nodded. "I'm not sure, but I noticed something that might help lead us to who they are."

"What's that?"

"Earlier in the year, I noticed something odd about Hazel. I wasn't sure what it was, then I realized she had a slight aura. I don't know how else to describe it. But it was there. It went away after I broke the spell, getting her out from José's control. I've seen that same aura around some students on campus in the last few weeks. Only—"

She hesitated, and the headmistress made a gesture with her hand, trying to encourage the words to come from Mia's mouth. "Only what, Mia?"

Mia sighed in frustration. "Only Marcus didn't have one. Ever. So maybe it doesn't have anything to do with the vampire thrall, and it's just a halfling feature? That's why I never said anything before."

Elmhurst shook her head. "No. That's not something halflings usually have. I absolutely think the aura you're describing has something to do with José and his control. It's strange that Marcus didn't have one, but it could be because of his compliance. The aura could suggest a person forced into servitude rather than one who willingly accepts it."

"Then we start with them. If we learned anything from Hazel, it should be that those forced into following the vampire's control are the most likely to want to get away from it. We should talk to them and find out what we can," Mia said.

"Until the bonds have been broken and Narco is no longer a threat to you, Mia, you are not to be alone. There are to be at least two people with you at all times," Elmhurst said.

"Yes, Headmistress," Mia said.

"I heard from Cassia today. She will be coming back to campus for a brief visit this week. She wants to check in on you," Elmhurst said.

"What did you tell her?" Mia asked.

"I've kept her informed of all developments. I know you don't want to worry her, but she is your guardian and deserves to know. She is also the best bounty hunter in the fae world. If there is anyone who can track down Narco, it will be her."

Mia nodded. Cassia had been hunting Narco since she had left campus but hadn't found him yet. And Cassia was becoming frustrated, but she wouldn't stop until the threat against Mia was eliminated. It made the young halfling feel more secure and confident, knowing her guardian was putting so much effort into finding the man who wanted to destroy her.

That sense of confidence was shattered two weeks later when the gargoyles appeared as the five met with Elmhurst to discuss a project they were working on. They were frantic as they told her of a portal that opened right outside the campus. The headmistress immediately went into action.

"Gather all the students," she said to the gargoyles. "Get all of them in the dining hall. Mia, you stay with me. The rest of you, find the students Mia has labeled as having the auras and bring them to the Mathematics Building. There will be a professor waiting to help you."

As Mia followed Elmhurst to the dining hall, the reality of what was happening finally settled in. It was tonight. All their preparations, anxiety, and watching, had led them to this. Her initial fear faded as the sense of duty and responsibility filled her. She was ready to defend herself, her school, and her friends.

Once the students streamed into the dining hall from their dorms and the few spots on campus where they were allowed after class, Elmhurst created a portal. She ushered the students through as quickly as they would go, sending them to another school. The headmaster of that school was waiting, ready to accept and care for them until Elmhurst sent for them again. Several of the staff monitored the students as they departed, and when the last one had left, Elmhurst asked if any were missing.

The staff read off the names of those who did not go through, and Mia mentally ticked off the ones who had the auras and should be waiting in the other building.

"Thank you," Elmhurst said. "Mia, come on."

They headed quickly for the Mathematics Building, a small structure in a corner of the main portion of campus.

"There are people missing," she said. "Ones who don't have the aura didn't go through the portal."

Elmhurst nodded. "They must be the ones who willingly went into servitude. Or those who are exceptionally weak-minded and didn't need the blood curse to become slaves."

"We had planned to release them of their curse this weekend," Mia said.

The headmistress nodded again. "I know. Either someone knew and tipped them off, or it is very unfortunate timing." They arrived at the building, but they didn't go inside.

"What are we going to do about them?" Mia asked. "The missing ones?"

"We can't do anything about them now. We have to prepare ourselves."

The doors to the building opened, and a small group of students tried to exit. Elmhurst approached the entrance and performed an enchantment to seal them in so no one could get in or out without knowing the specific spell.

Mia saw Hazel coming toward her from another building. "Hazel, what are you doing? You should have gone through the portal to the other school."

"No, Mia." Hazel shook her head adamantly. "I'm not leaving you. I want to help."

"It's not safe," Mia argued.

"I don't care. You took care of me. You protected me, and you freed me. You were there for me when I needed you, and I'm doing the same."

"We all are."

Mia turned to Cinder, who had appeared from behind the legs of the Scooby Gang.

"All of us," Dan said as the gargoyles flew into place with them.

Mia's heart swelled as she looked at the group in front of her. There was no question in any of their eyes, no hesitation. They were going to stay and face this with her.

"Mia," Elmhurst said. Mia glanced at the headmistress, who was staring across the grounds. "They're here."

CHAPTER TWENTY-NINE

The sheer size of the crowd crossing the grounds in their direction was dizzying. Mia had anticipated José and a few of his servants. She had thought she might have to face a few of the creatures she had encountered during her time in Shanghai. But she didn't expect the army coming her way.

A clan of a dozen wolf shifters walked beside several fae and two intense-looking witches. But it was the massive wall of vampires that took her breath away. Narco himself was leading the march.

"It's José's family," Hazel murmured. "His closest allies."

"He has dhampirs with him," Luna pointed out.

Mia noticed the five dhampirs interspersed among the true vampires. Even bolstered by the teachers and staff who weren't guarding the enthralled students, her group felt incredibly small. But that didn't lessen their strength. José's group had numbers and definite power, but they didn't know what they were coming up against. He didn't truly know what he was messing with when it came to Mia, or to the group of five. It was time for them to show him.

They rushed toward José, and his army advanced. The two groups clashed in the middle, and the battle began.

"Mia!" a voice shouted.

One of the professors stood a few feet away. He tossed her a set of weapons, and when it fell into her hands, she felt anchored. It was a pair of sai, a three-pronged weapon she had learned to use while training for Wushu. The blades were the ideal weapon for women, easy for her to control, and familiar in her hands.

She wielded them powerfully as she ran headlong toward a cluster of vampires. Sending up a temporary shield around herself to protect herself from their attacks, she swung each sai so they sliced right through the necks of the vampires. They paused, their eyes widening as they registered what she had done. Mia didn't hesitate. She cut through again, separating their heads from their shoulders. They bobbed for a moment, and toppled backward and onto the ground.

Mia didn't give herself the time to revel in the triumph. They were small, young, and weak. It wouldn't be so easy moving forward, and there was far more to be done. Around her, the grounds rang with the sounds of battle. Shouts and cries rose up into the night air, and the coppery smell of blood burned in her throat.

Ahead of Mia, a shifter leapt forward, transformed into a vicious wolf in midair, and bared his dripping fangs at her. She braced herself for the fight, but before the creature reached her, a large boulder fell from the sky and crushed it to the ground. The sound of bones cracking marked the shifter's immediate death.

Mia looked up at Dan, who hovered above. Steve floated behind him, holding another huge boulder, poised to drop it on a fae man below. Mia flashed him a grin and surged back into the fight.

One of the witches had Zander on the ground, and vines had come up from the soil to entangle him. They wrapped tightly around his body, held him to the ground, and wound around him to his throat. The witch laughed darkly as she controlled the vines. Zander managed to move his hand enough to send a blast of magic at her.

The witch stumbled away, but she stepped forward again and pointed at the ground near him. Another thicker vine burst from the ground, splitting the dirt and grass as it came. Covered in barbed thorns, it joined the other in encircling Zander's body. The Seelie boy gritted his teeth against the pain, refusing to give her the satisfaction of watching him scream, but Mia could see the blood.

The sight of her friend bleeding infuriated her. She lunged toward the witch just as Zander sent new magic through the vines that began to shrivel them. Before the witch could do anything, Mia thrust one sai through the woman's chest. The witch gagged and fell to the ground.

Mia wrenched the sai from her body and looked at the thick, dark blood running down the middle blade down toward the two smaller ones that came from either side. The grotesque woman groaned again before she sagged to the ground.

The instant she died, the shriveled vines pulled away from Zander. He fought the rest of the way out of them, and Mia reached for his hand to help him up.

"Thanks," he said.

"Of course. She doesn't know what she's dealing with," Mia said.

"Better believe it. I bet she had no idea I have previous experience fighting for my life against vines."

Mia stared at Zander strangely, but he lifted his sword to ready himself and shrugged. "Ask Vivi about it sometime."

He ran toward Carson, who was battling against two shifters, and Mia watched them combine their magic to kill both creatures in a single blast. Suddenly she felt a breath on the back of her neck, and she spun around.

One of the older, stronger vampires stood close behind her.

She slashed her blade across his neck, but the weapon barely made a mark. The vampire laughed and stepped closer to her. He reached out, but before his hands could touch her, Mia slammed the sai blade into his chest.

It wouldn't kill him. But as she had hoped, the injury paralyzed him long enough for her to force him to the ground and pin him down to cut off his head. As soon as she moved away, Cinder came rushing from between the legs of a fae woman nearby and set the vampire's corpse aflame.

The longer they fought, the more brutal and intense the battle became. Blood ran down her arms, her vision blurred, and parts of her body were aching from injuries she didn't have time to check yet.

Mia blasted out her magic. She used every skill she could, putting every bit of focus and concentration on controlling what she was doing. A shockwave wiped out several vampires, and they tumbled to the ground at Carson's feet. He met her eyes.

"Maybe it's time for a little change of weather," he said with a wink.

She nodded, and they ran to find the rest of the Scooby Gang. All together, they made a plan and spread out. Conjuring a strong wind, Mia concentrated it into one strong ball and sent it across the battlefield to Zander. He spread it out a little and threw it through a group of fae to Carson. The fae were torn apart by the strength of the air and landed in a tangled mass on the ground. Mia and the two boys tossed the wind around, occasionally adding new magic and enchantments to further decimate the numbers standing against them.

They fought for what felt like hours, but finally, the enemy's numbers dwindled. Nearly all were dead. But not enough.

Mia turned from the final vampire she had killed and saw José right behind Hazel. She tried to pull Hazel away with her thoughts, but it didn't work. They were across the field from her, and Mia wondered if distance played a part, or if it was because she was so exhausted. Mia ran, wanting to snatch the girl away from him before he could bite her.

Bending her head back and to the side, exposing her neck, José sank his fangs into her and took deep gulps. Mia screamed out. Anger and hurt rushed through her as she realized that not being fully able to control her powers had cost Hazel her life. With the way José was drinking, Mia wasn't going to get there in time.

Her hands lifted, and glowing streams of magic burst from the six points of the sai weapons she held. Each burrowed into a fae or shifter nearby, instantly wiping out six of the few still remaining.

Narco stared at the carnage before he fled. The moment she'd killed half a dozen of his warriors, he knew he didn't stand a chance against Mia and her friends. None of the reports he'd received had said she'd possessed anywhere near this level of power. A strategic retreat was his only option at this point. It would make it possible for him to live to fight another day.

José didn't have the same compulsion. He wanted to stay and fight Mia, to be able to prove his bravery and his loyalty to Narco. Besides, he thought she would have used up too much of her power and be exhausted by this point. Killing her would be easy, and he could have his reward at last. It didn't matter what she tried with her blades. Lightning didn't kill vampires. It hurt a lot, but it didn't actually kill them.

The blood lust a vampire experienced in the middle of a large battle didn't help his sense of self-preservation, either.

And all that was left were vampires, José and his brother, Miguel. Mia cried out, channeling every bit of her anger and sadness at the vampires. Miguel instantly dropped to the ground, his head exploding. José came running at her, but Mia held up her hand, causing him to skid to a stop. It all came down to him. He was the last of his family left to fight. The field around them was littered with the bodies of the vampires and other species they had brought with them, but Mia also recognized the faces of a few fallen teachers from the academy.

Tears streamed down her face as she lifted her hand, pulling José from his feet with her magic so he hovered a couple inches off the ground. She clenched her hand, turning her grip into a magical vice that would slowly crush José to death.

Cassia ran to her side and put a hand on her shoulder. "Stop," she said. "Mia, stop. We need him for questioning. He'll be brought in and interrogated so we can find out as much about him and this operation as we can."

Elmhurst stepped forward and performed an enchantment. A jail cell appeared, and Mia forced José into it. When he was inside, she released the grip, and he fell to the ground in a heap. The headmistress went inside and checked him.

"He's not dead. At least, not for a vampire," she confirmed.

They brought him to an underground facility for interrogation, but they wouldn't allow Mia inside. She waited impatiently, and finally, Cassia emerged from the questioning to talk to her.

"What's going on?" Mia asked.

"The interrogation is over," Cassia said. "And it was interesting. It turns out that a certain fae believes you are a descendant of the royal line. It was once believed that this line of the family was extinct."

"Who? And what royal line?" Mia asked.

"José didn't know who Narco's working for," Headmistress Elmhurst answered.

"But, what about me being descended from royalty? How's that even possible?" Mia ran a hand through her messy hair and looked frantically between Cassia and Elmhurst.

Mia had zero desire to be royal. She'd seen how royals in Great Britain were treated, and she wanted none of it. Sure, in fairy tales, it always worked out in the end, but not in real life. And from what she knew about fae, it would be much worse for her than it ever was for the Duchess of Sussex, and she only married into a human royal family. Being a halfling descent of a fae princess had to be worse than an apocalypse.

Headmistress Elmhurst put her hands up in a placating gesture. "Don't worry, Mia. I doubt you are who they think you are."

"It must be possible if so many are after me." Mia began to pace the small room.

Cassia nodded. "While it is possible, it's not definite."

"At one time, the fae realm was controlled by one Court. The king and queen of the fae Court had three daughters. The two older princesses agreed to kill their parents and split the realm and share leadership thousands of years ago. Princess Violet, the youngest daughter, is dead. Not a lot is known about Princess Violet as her sisters tried to make everyone forget she was ever alive." The bounty hunter gave her charge a light hug.

Mia pulled herself from Cassia's embrace. "How does a dead princess from thousands of years ago affect me? If we are even related." She threw her hands in the air.

Cassia ran a hand down her face and sighed. "It's possible you're one of her descendants. You'd be a very long way down the family tree, of course, but that could explain what you are capable of doing. Even though you're a halfling, you have very powerful fae blood in you. That enables you to do things no one expects you to be able to do."

"Could I ever be a fae princess?" Mia asked.

Cassia shook her head. "No. Even if we believe what José said, it wouldn't be possible because you are a halfling. The fae would never accept you as royal or recognize your right to rule. Besides, neither of the queens would give up their throne. There are only two Courts, so there is no throne to be had."

"And if I disagree with that?" Mia asked.

"The queens are far too powerful for you to beat. And even if you did manage to beat one, there is still the other. She would come at you with absolutely everything and defeat you so she could be Queen of all Fae. The Courts would merge. Nobody wants that. There would be a war like nothing Earth has ever seen if the two Courts were forced to merge."

Mia nodded, her mind churning with questions and options. She didn't know how to move forward or what to do next. Should she try to take over one of the Courts and claim a throne? Perhaps try to take over both?

No. She didn't want to rule anything. That was far too much pressure and responsibility, not to mention the possibility of a civil war amongst the fae. Besides, she may not even be the descendant of Princess Violet. Although she doubted so many would be after her if she wasn't. Most likely, she was.

But that didn't change the fact that she couldn't simply accept people coming after her all the time. She had to keep herself and everyone around her safe. Perhaps she should go into hiding.

Whatever she was going to do, she needed to make a choice, and soon. The lives of so many depended on how she decided to move forward.

The story continues with book three, The Emerald Portal, *coming soon to Amazon and Kindle Unlimited.*

Want more books by J.L. Hendricks?

Check out Miss Claus and Her Secret Santa for a fun and exciting new take on who Santa Claus really is! Did you know he was an Arctic Wolf shifter? You didn't? Then you gotta check out this completed series today!

Miss Claus and Her Secret Santa

AUTHOR NOTES J.L. HENDRICKS
SEPTEMBER 4, 2020

Thank you so very much for picking up book 2, The Forbidden Portal, and reading all the way back here. I hope you are enjoying Mia's adventures and discovering along with her the perils and joys of her magical abilities. I know I did when I wrote it.

This book was written right after my first trip to Scotland, and Michael and I were able to meet up in person, since we were both there for a 20Books conference. The magic of Scotland and its beauty is going to be portrayed in book 3. In fact, it's going to be a huge part of book 3. I've always enjoyed including scenes from my various world travels to books I create. This series is no different. I've been to Paris and the Louvre, and right now as I write this note, I'm in Montana. I'm actually here for a month scouting the state for locations of current books as well as future books.

Montana is a beautiful state full of so many glorious settings for books. I actually had a dream about a dragon here in Montana that's most likely going to become a new book for me. I've been chatting about it with my newsletter subscribers. If you want to hear more about my version of a dragon rider, then be sure to subscribe to my newsletter, where I do share about my writing adventures as well as give away prequels to existing series.

In fact, Mike and I are working on a prequel for The Unwanted Princess Trilogy. We are going to give more backstory of Mia's ancestry, and some of Cassia's, too. Those on my Newsletter will hear about it first, and might even get a sneak peek.

Next up for Mia is the Slamball World Championships, something like the Olympics. It only happens every 4 years, and this time it's taking place on an island in Scotland! We are also going to take a trip to the faerie pools on the Isle of Sky. I went there and one of the scenes in book 3, The Forbidden Portal, is something I came up with while hiking to the pools. I can't wait for you to read the final book in this trilogy and let me know what you think!

Remember, it's the reviews and emails that let authors know what you think about their stories. So please, don't forget to leave a review of the books in the Unwanted Princess Trilogy today.

And I also want to thank Michael and everyone at LMBPN for their help with this second book. Each time I'm amazed at the wonderful beta readers, JIT readers, and editors. Also, the cover designer did a fantastic job! I am totally loving this series of covers, what do you think? I'd love to know what your thoughts are on these covers.

Thank you,

Jen

ABOUT J.L. HENDRICKS

J.L. Hendricks is a USA Today Bestselling independent author who enjoys many genres, as evidenced by her catalogue of available books. She is currently focused on Clean & Wholesome Romance and Urban Fantasy, but has also written Space Opera, LitRPG, Paranormal, and Christmas books.

This past year has been spent researching the Clean & Wholesome genre for her new pen name, Jenna Hendricks. She also just finished writing an Academy Urban Fantasy series with a very exciting name in the Indie Publishing world.

One thing she learned early on is to accept help from others in the Indie world, and she is very grateful to those who have helped her along the way! The Indie publishing world is full of extremely nice and helpful authors, which is what makes this the best job she's ever had.

In early 2016 she decided to finally write, and finish a book, because of a few friends who encouraged her to do so. She hopes her stories entertain you and can bring a laugh on occasion.

Actually, it was her roommate's cat who talked her into staying at home to be her minion all day long! Pyper truly believes that J.L. is here to serve her alone.

Come and chat with J.L. on Facebook at:
https://www.facebook.com/JLHendricksAuthor/

And check out her Amazon author page at:
http://jlhendricksauthor.com/62fp

But don't forget her website and blog at:
https://jlhendricksauthor.com/

OTHER BOOKS BY J.L. HENDRICKS

New Orleans Magic

Book 0: Magic's Not Real
Book 1: New Orleans Magic
Book 2: Hurricane of Magic
Book 3: Council of Magic

Worlds Away Series
Book 0: Worlds Revealed (join my Newsletter to get this exclusive freebie)
Book 1: Worlds Away
Book 2: Worlds Collide
Book 2.5: Worlds Explode
Book 3: Worlds Entwined

A Shifter Christmas Romance Series
Book 0: Santa Meets Mrs. Claus
Book 1: Miss Claus and the Secret Santa
Book 2: Miss Claus under the Mistletoe
Book 3: Miss Claus and the Christmas Wedding

Book 4: Miss Claus and Her Polar Opposite

The FBI Dragon Chronicles
Book 1: A Ritual of Fire
Book 2: A Ritual of Death
Book 3: A Ritual of Conquest

Chronicles Of The Unwanted Princess
(with Michael Anderle)
Book 1: The Portal of Chance
Book 2: The Forbidden Portal
Book 3: The Emerald Portal

See these titles and more at https://www.jlhendricksauthor.com/

CONNECT WITH THE AUTHORS

Connect with J.L. Hendricks

Facebook:
https://www.facebook.com/JLHendricksAuthor/

Amazon:
http://jlhendricksauthor.com/62fp

Website:
https://jlhendricksauthor.com/

Connect with Michael Anderle

Website: http://lmbpn.com

Email List: http://lmbpn.com/email/

Social Media:

https://www.facebook.com/LMBPNPublishing

https://twitter.com/lmbpn

https://www.instagram.com/lmbpn_publishing/

https://www.bookbub.com/authors/michael-anderle